Bear

ISBN-13: 978-1540757432
ISBN-10: 1540757439
Copyright © 2015, T. S. Joyce
First electronic publication: May 2015

T. S. Joyce
www. tsjoyce.com

NOTE FROM THE AUTHOR:

This book is a work of fiction. The names, characters, places, and incidents are products of the writer's imagination or have been used fictitiously and are not to be construed as real. Any resemblance to persons, living or dead, actual events, locale or organizations is entirely coincidental. The author does not have any control over and does not assume any responsibility for third-party websites or their content.

Published in the United States of America

First digital publication: May 2015
First print publication: December 2016

Editing: Corinne DeMaagd

ONE

Driving along Main Street, Dade Keller scratched behind the ear of the mutt sitting beside him in the passenger seat of his truck. Usually, he made Tank ride in the bed of his pickup, but today he'd taken pity on him and gave him a window seat. Tank was the firehouse's mascot. Dade had meant to adopt a brave dog for the firehouse mascot, but Tank couldn't even handle a yearly trip to the vet without losing his shit. A few shots in his furry butt made him howl like someone was ax murdering him.

Rubbing the brindle, short-haired hound-mix on the head, Dade muttered, "You know, if you stay still for the vet, we'll get out of there in half an hour tops. You don't have to make it traumatic for everyone involved."

Tank cocked his head and slurped his panting tongue back in his mouth. One of his bottom canines caught on his lip. A honk sounded behind him and Dade waved an apology, then eased through the stale green light. Tank lived up at Fire Station 6 where Dade worked, but for some reason, he was always the one recruited for the dog's annual vet check-ups. He didn't really mind, though. He had a day off and nothing planned, and besides, he'd bonded with Tank over the two years he'd lived at the firehouse. As much as he hated admitting he had an attachment to anything, he loved that Tank followed him around and no one else when he was working his forty-eight hour shifts.

Secretly, he thought of Tank as his, but if he muttered that little gem out loud, Boone, one of his older brothers, would rib him relentlessly for going soft. And dammit, he was about as soft as a porcupine. IESA had done that—made him into a black ops weapon incapable of attaching to anyone. A vision of that day in the barn after Krueger had kidnapped Cody's mate, Rory, played across his mind, and he winced. The memory caused him to touch the acid burn scars across his neck. A reminder that humans couldn't be trusted with secrets.

A black sedan slid in behind him as he headed toward the vet clinic at the end of the main drag in Breckenridge. Dade narrowed his eyes in the rearview mirror at the familiar car.

It couldn't be. Shayna couldn't possibly be that dumb.

Dark, tinted windows hid the driver, but as he took the next right, the car behind him sped up and rode inches from his bumper.

"Shit," Dade muttered, turning left onto a wooded dirt road. Tank growled. Nothing in Dade wanted to do this now, or ever, and he stifled his own snarl that softly rattled his chest. "Tell me about it, boy."

He pulled off onto the shoulder and slid out of his truck, slammed the door behind him. Hooking his hands on his hips, he waited as Shayna took her time getting out of the sedan in sky-high heels and a short black skirt that was created to lure men to their deaths. This chick was a black widow if he'd ever seen one, and right now, with her brunette waves tickling her low neck line, lips painted red, and that

7

cold, devil-may-care smile plastered on her face, she looked like a right proper little man-eater.

"What do you want, Shayna?"

Inside the truck, Tank was going mad, barking and lunging at the door. Impressive, since Tank liked everyone. Dade's regard for the IESA operative sank further, if that was even possible.

"You know, when I went back to check on our little operation in the woods, all I found was a torched barn."

"I don't know what you're talking about, but if I did, I'd say I regret that you weren't there for the fireworks show." Because Damon Daye would've definitely made sure she wasn't here to blackmail shifters anymore.

"You fucked me once." She leaned on the side of his truck and offered him a smile that failed to reach her eyes.

"I was drunk, and that was before I knew who you really were."

"I want seconds."

His single, humorless laugh cracked across the quiet woods. "That's a hell no. Have a nice life, Shayna." He turned and reached for his door handle, but she yanked him back with a strength she shouldn't have possessed.

He swung around, but her eyes had changed from their emerald color to a churning silver. "What have you done?" he asked on a breath, dread slamming into him.

"It's not what I did, but what one of your kind did for me. Everyone has a price."

"I don't."

"Yes you do, Dade. Because I know who you're sleeping with these days."

"What are you talking about?"

"Lisa Warren."

He took a step back from Shayna. "Who?"

Her eyes tightened and roiled like mercury. "I saw you leave her house last week."

"The woman from the bar?"

Shayna drew up short. "You're with her," she said, less certain this time.

"Crazy woman, listen carefully. I'm not *with* anyone. I'm not looking for a mate, and I'm sure as shit not looking for a casual fuck from a woman who works for IESA and has made my life a living hell. Now kindly piss off. I have somewhere to be."

"I need a cub."

"What?" He rounded on her, heart pounding with fury. "You would make a terrible mother."

"I don't give a shit about being a mother, you idiot. In light of Krueger's unfortunate disappearance along with our men, IESA is rebuilding. Aw, look at your sad face." Shayna pouted out her bottom lip. "Did you think your little killing spree was going to make the government forget about you? Krueger's work needs to go on. You and your brothers were at the end of your usefulness on missions. You got too nosey and grew some morals. We lured you to the barn to take you for reproductive research, but you ruined our attempt to save at least some of you, you ungrateful dick. If you won't be forced, I'll buy you instead."

"I'm taking a hard pass on this one, Shayna." Dade's voice cracked like a whip, but he didn't care. He wanted nothing more than to strangle the woman for all the pain she'd brought. And now she was a fucking bear shifter, like him.

"I have agreed to bear a cub and was given a choice between you and your brothers for the other half of my future cub's genetic material. IESA wants the Keller line, and since Gage won't even look at me, and Cody is shacked up with that whore now, it's between you and Boone. And quite honestly, you're the better lay."

Bile crept up Dade's throat at the thought of her sleeping with Boone, too. It seemed the Keller boys had all been screwed. "I won't be bought. Not by you or anyone else."

"But you were fine with being blackmailed. When your family was in danger, you all flocked to do our bidding. Don't make me go down that road again." She turned and lowered his tailgate, then leaned on it and pulled her skirt up to expose her bare ass. She arched her back until he could see her pink, wet lips between her legs. "Now hurry, Dade. I'm ovulating."

Dade looked around the woods, shocked. "This is what you want? A quickie fuck on the side of the road?"

"Well, no. I want lots of quickie fucks, lover. At least until you put a cub in me. Lucky you."

"You're crazy," he whispered, disgusted.

"Oh, come on. You didn't even know Lisa's name. At least you know who you're sleeping with this

11

time."

He huffed a blast of air and shook his head. "The answer is never. Now get off my truck before you give it an STD."

Shayna spun, eyes blazing. "You'll do this, or your entire family will pay. Anyone you get close to will have to look over their shoulder. IESA is coming for you, Dade. I was the one who convinced my superiors you were more useful to us alive than dead. I was the one who petitioned to have you spared for reproductive research after Krueger went missing. The only thing standing in between the Breck Crew and complete annihilation is me. You pissed off everyone when you killed Krueger and half of our damned corporation."

"I don't know what you're talking about."

"Liar!"

"You kidnapped Rory, tried to kill me, tried to take my brother's for some fucked up science experiment, and IESA's treachery backfired. If your people are missing, seems to me the blame lies with your agency. Not with me or my crew."

"You're monsters, Dade! Look at you! Look at your eyes, all gold and green and couldn't pass for human if you tried. We can do whatever we want with you because you are monsters. What would the public do if we told them what we're really protecting them from?"

"That's bullshit. We aren't dangerous to humans."

"And who do you think they're going to trust on that, huh? Some savage bear shifters, or the people entrusted to protect the public at all costs? Accept it Dade. I run your life."

Screw the open tailgate, he couldn't stand here and listen to this anymore. He hopped into his truck and rolled the window down as he turned the engine. "The only monster here is you, Shayna. My answer stands."

"I own you!" she screeched as he spun the truck around her, kicking up dust with his tires.

Tank scrabbled toward the open window, snarling and barking at the woman who stood in the cloud of dust with her skirt up to her stomach.

Dade slammed his fist against the steering wheel and gritted his teeth until his face hurt.

Shayna was wrong.

No one owned him.

A couple more miles, and he pulled into the parking lot of the veterinary clinic, pissed as hell and ready to crack some skulls. Shayna was trouble, but as tempting as it was to use the skills he'd obtained from IESA's forced missions on that woman, he couldn't just go around killing everyone who threatened the Breck Crew. There had to be a better way to get IESA off their backs. He pulled his phone from the cup holder and texted Boone and Cody.

Shayna's back, and someone's Changed her.

His phone was probably bugged, but screw it. Whoever was tracking his messages already knew what he was and likely knew what Shayna was, too. Shoving the cell in his back pocket, he grabbed Tank's leash and slid out of the truck with the dog following directly.

His cell buzzed back, but he ignored it. He'd meet up with his brothers tonight at the station and figure out their next move. For now, he was going to put a pair of sunglasses over his blazing eyes and get Tank through his exam, all while trying not to rip anyone's head off.

TWO

"Are you sure you're okay?" Dr. Voss asked.

Quinn Copeland nodded her head and swallowed the sob in her throat. "I'm fine. Really."

"The first time is the hardest." Dr. Voss's sad blue eyes bore into Quinn as she sidestepped out of the room.

"I'm just going to take a moment before I get to the next patient," Quinn said with as much of a smile as she could muster. It came out a lip tremble, so she didn't wait to see Dr. Voss's reaction to her obvious weakness. She just turned and left the room without another word.

Geez, she was so not cut out for this. Her face crumpled, and she rushed into an empty room before the other vet tech could see her breakdown. She'd taken the courses and gotten a job here because she had wanted to help pets, not kill them. Okay, the poor dog, Daphne, was too far gone and in such pain, but still. Witnessing the end to her life was heartbreaking.

And her owner had sobbed the entire time, snuggling the little poodle until long after it had drawn its last breath.

Quinn slid down the wall of the empty room, shoulders shaking as the water works really began. Poor little Daphne. And her owner! She would go home tonight without her pet, and it would be awful. Just thinking about something happening to one of her own dogs brought on another wave of grief.

She hiccupped and drew her knees up to her chest, then rested her face on her forearms.

When the door burst open, Quinn looked up and froze as a giant man dragged a whimpering dog inside.

"Stop being such a pussy, Tank," the man growled out, pulling on the leash as the dog locked his legs.

His nails scrabbled on the tile floors as the man

got him past the door and closed it behind him. He turned and Quinn gasped.

From her place on the floor, it looked like his head was almost touching the ceiling. His jaw was covered in short, blond stubble, but not the unkempt kind. The designer kind that belonged on billboard models. Chiseled jaw and lips set in a grim line, he jerked to a stop as he spied her sitting on the floor like a weirdo.

"Oh, God," he whispered, as if he'd stumbled upon a king cobra instead of a crying woman. "I'm so sorry. The lady at the desk said room three. This is room three, right?" He was backing slowly toward the door, his work boots echoing across the tile with every powerful step.

"No, it's fine. You're in the right place." When she realized she was staring at a horrific scar across his neck, she forced herself to look away. Except when she did, her gaze traveled down the perfect indented line between his pecs exposed by his gray V-neck shirt. The thin cotton fabric clung to his sculpted torso before the shirt loosened and hung over his light-washed, holey-knee jeans.

Intimidated, she stood clumsily and wiped her

tear-stained cheeks. The blush in her face was burning up to her ears now, and she cursed her fair skin. "Is he here for a check-up?"

"Yeah, but you can't tell from the way he's acting. He always bawls like a baby during his annual visit, like we're putting him to sleep or something."

The mention of putting anything to sleep conjured a vision of the owner leaning over her poodle, crying as the little elderly dog took its last breath, and the imaginings buckled her. Overwhelmed with emotion, Quinn spun and left the room. But when she went out to the hall, Dr. Voss was talking to the other vet tech, and Quinn slunk back into the room, completely trapped.

"Are you okay?" The Sasquatch was hovering in the corner like a phantom now, and behind his reflective sunglasses, his face had taken on a combined look of terror and acute suspicion. Tears did that to men.

"This is so unprofessional. I'm sorry." Quinn grabbed a box of tissues from beside a jar of dog biscuits and yanked out three before blotting her weepy face. "I just started this job, and I took it to help animals, and now..."

"What happened?" the man asked, voice softer now as he let his dog's leash slip from his hand.

"I can't talk about it," she rasped out, throat thickening with emotion.

"Okay. Shit." He didn't seem to know what to do with his hands. "Okay," he repeated. He straightened his spine and jerked his attention to the door. "Someone's coming."

"What?"

"Will you get fired for crying?" He looked so confused.

And now she was confused. "I don't think so. I don't know."

"Here," he rushed out. He snatched up his dog and put the poor frozen critter up on the table.

Quinn gasped when she saw her monstrous reflection in the man's aviator sunglasses. Raccoon eyes thanks to the double helping of mascara she'd used this morning and her nose was as red as Rudolph's. Which would be fine if she wasn't staring into this sexy Adonis's face.

The door behind her opened, just like the man had said it would, and she jumped. The man's giant hand clamped on her upper arm when she began to turn, stopping her.

"So, you see, I think it's his diet." The stranger gave a friendly smile to whoever had just wandered into the room.

"Quinn, are you taking this one?" Gertie, the other vet tech asked. "I could've sworn Dr. Voss told me to take room three."

"I want Quinn," the man said in a tone that brokered no arguing.

A chill washed over her skin at the authority in his words. No longer was he the man fighting for dominance with a scared hound mix who was apparently afraid of weeping women. Now, he was a man who knew his place in the world and expected others to react accordingly.

"Right," Gertie said. "I'll just get the next one then."

When the door clicked softly closed, Quinn let off a sigh of relief. "I'm so sorry, sir."

"Dade."

"I'm so sorry, Dade. This is not at all how this clinic is run. I'm just... I don't know what I'm doing here."

"Did a pet die?"

She nodded miserably.

Dade took off his sunglasses. His eyes were the color of the ocean, blue and green, and gentle as he clutched his dog to his chest. "You're a soft-hearted little thing, aren't you?"

For some reason, it made her stomach lurch to nod her head yes. Dade didn't seem the type of man who had much use for soft-hearted things. Which was a stupid thought because she wasn't exactly a part of his life. She didn't even know the man.

Petting his scared pooch, she said, "You know, pussies, if you're speaking of cats, are actually quite tough."

Dade's blond brows lowered. "Huh?"

"You told your dog to stop being a pussy when you dragged him in here." She scratched the dog behind the ears. "And you're not a pussy, are you big fella?" She dipped her voice to the one she used with her own two Yorkshire Terriers at home. "You're a big tough guy, just like your daddy."

"Oh, he's not my... You think I'm a tough guy?"

Heat filled her cheeks when he paid her such direct attention. She'd never been good at speaking to people. Chronic shyness made social interaction awkward at best, which was the main reason she worked with animals. She connected with them in a way she hadn't ever been able to understand people. "Am I wrong?"

His nostrils flared as he inhaled slowly and studied her. "You have no idea how right you are."

Another chill brushed up her skin, and she dropped her eyes, unable to hold his clear aquamarine gaze. He was pointing out how dissimilar they were. She got it. She just didn't understand why he felt the need to put them on two different planes.

"Right, let's get this guy checked out then, shall we? What's his name?"

"Tank."

She tried to ignore Dade's attention as she ran a thorough check-up on Tank. The hound relaxed as she petted and talked to him, but when she left and came back with the trio of shots he needed, the dog started whimpering before she even uncapped the needles.

Dr. Voss opened the door, but as soon as she saw the dog, she nodded knowingly and waved her clipboard at Dade. "Good to see you and Tank again. I'll be in shortly to do his final evaluation and give you his heartworm prevention."

"'K," Dade said, his focus still on Quinn.

It was unsettling how intense the man was. Soft one moment and distant the next. She couldn't get a good read on him.

She lined up the needle as Dade held Tank, but the wailing was getting to her, tugging at her heartstrings. She didn't want to hurt him, especially not now when she was emotionally ragged after witnessing the poodle pass away. She hesitated, needle hovering over Tank's fur.

"It's okay," Dade whispered, encasing her hand in his.

Warmth flooded her knuckles under his touch.

"I'll help," he murmured, then pushed her hand.

Tank howled, and she rushed the last two shots without assistance to avoid the strange tingling sensation that had taken over her skin where Dade had touched her. He took Tank off the exam table, and she gave him a couple of dog treats from the jar. The poor hound slunk around the room, chewing his treaties with his tail between his legs.

Quinn tried and failed to meet Dade's gaze, then tried again and gave him a smile. "Thanks for earlier.

When you covered for me with the other vet tech. That was nice of you."

"I'm not nice," he said, slipping his sunglasses back over his eyes.

Dr. Voss bustled through the door. With a squeeze of her hand, she whispered near her ear, "You can take the rest of the day off."

"But really, I'm okay."

"It's only an hour early, and you've earned it. Gertie and I can handle the rest of the appointments today."

Disappointed in herself, Quinn nodded. She dared a glance at Dade, and he was watching her with a troubled quirk to his light brows, as if he'd heard Dr. Voss dismiss her, which was impossible from across the room.

Flustered, she turned and left, closing the door behind her.

Whether that man was soft or tough, nice or not, Quinn's instincts screamed that Dade was trouble.

Quinn made her way to the small locker where she kept her things, then pulled her satchel from inside and slung it over her chest. With a wave to Gertie, she made her way out the back exit and pulled the lock off her bike. She had a car, but she only lived a mile away from the clinic and liked to bike when the weather was fair. New to town, she was still enamored with how fresh the air smelled here at the edge of the Colorado Rockies. But when she swung her leg over and began to pedal, the bike wasn't moving as smoothly as it usually did.

She dismounted and groaned as she beheld the flat back tire. Today sucked. Holding back another wave of pathetic tears, she pushed her jouncing bike toward the small, two-lane road that would lead her home.

She'd almost made it to Main Street when the sound of a car drew her attention behind her. A forest green Tacoma with giant black rims coasted up beside her. Dade sat behind the wheel and lowered his sunglasses. "Gotta flat?"

Quinn wiped her eyes and cleared her throat. Timidly, she said, "I don't usually cry every minute of my life, you know. You've just caught me on a bad day."

"I can see that." Dade looked around, and his eyes settled on a black sedan that was parked on the side of the road. The look he gave that car was downright venomous before he turned back to Quinn. "Good luck getting home."

His voice had gone cold and empty, and a little noise of indignation crawled up the back of her throat as he sped off. What a jerk. She'd thought he was about to ask her if she wanted a ride home, but nope. He was just stopping so he could kick gravel up at her as he drove away.

Any nice thoughts about the man flitted away as she watched him disappear in a cloud of dust.

THREE

"Dade. Dade!" Cody said, slamming his hand on the table. "Are you even listening?"

Station 6 was quiet tonight, which was fine because Boone, Gage, and Cody were the only ones on shift. Breckenridge had three stations around the area, but this one was the biggest, and usually the busiest. Not tonight, though. Like the calm before a storm, the quiet had the hairs lifting on the back of Dade's neck.

"Yeah, man, I'm listening," he muttered, setting down the napkin he'd been shredding. Really, he'd been thinking of Quinn and the way Shayna had watched them when he'd pulled up beside Quinn on the side of the road earlier today.

27

"Then what do you think we should do?" Gage asked.

Boone narrowed his eyes at him, but it was Cody's look of utter frustration that held Dade's attention. He pet Tank's head as the dog rested it on his thigh. "I don't think we should go public. It isn't just us it affects, Cody. What about the Ashe Crew, the Gray Backs, the Boarlanders? Hell, what about every crew across the world? Our decision to expose what we are puts all shifters at risk. Not just the Breck Crew and not just bear shifters." Dade shook his head and leaned back in the plastic chair. "It doesn't feel right. Not right now."

"Okay, so we let Shayna rebuild IESA. We do nothing. We leave them with all the cards and start giving into blackmail again. We allow them to use the cubs, Ma, our mates as pawns in a game that will end up with us all dead. Is that what you're suggesting?"

"No, Cody," Dade gritted out. "I just think we need to take more time to think about this. About what coming out to the public will really mean. We'll be shunned or strung up to the nearest tree and burned. How does that make the cubs any safer? How does that make our family any better off?"

"But if we admit what we are, it takes the power away from IESA and puts our fate in the public's hands."

Dade sighed and crossed his arms over his chest. "You're alpha, Cody. You get to make the final decision, but I'm not on board. It comes down to who we can trust with our safety. IESA or humans. At least IESA has a reason to keep us alive."

"Which is?"

Experimentation, black ops missions, secret weapons. Shit. All of those answers felt like acid in his throat, so he just shook his head and shrugged. "I'll back whatever decision you make, but I think you need to call the other crews we know and hear advice from them before we go public. If they say no, we should consider their answer. They have a stake in this decision, too."

"You realize us going public and outing IESA gives us a safety net, right?" Boone asked. "They won't be able to push us around anymore. They've sent us all to war, pinned us unknowingly against our own kind. How many did they have us kill before we figured out our targets weren't terrorists? They kidnapped Rory and tagged us with acid-filled trackers, Dade. No one knows the burn of that more than you and Cody."

At the mention of the capsule Krueger had detonated in his neck, the one meant to end his life, the skin on his throat seared. He dropped his gaze to Cody's ruined hand. His older brother had been trying to rip the tracker out of his neck when Krueger hit that kill switch, and they'd both been marred. Yeah, the price the Keller family had paid was great, and he didn't want to be at IESA's mercy again, but every generation of shifters since the beginning of time had remained hidden for a reason.

Humans couldn't be trusted any more than IESA.

Dade rubbed his forehead to ward off an oncoming headache. "You have my answer on it. I vote no. I vote we wait and see if Shayna is as efficient at killing as Krueger was. We already wiped out most of IESA once. We can do it again."

"They're cockroaches, and you know it," Cody said softly, eyes on his clasped hands resting on the table in front of him. "We killed a few, thanks to Damon Daye and Bruiser. Sheer dumb luck on the timing because we should all be in a shallow grave right now or penned up in some cage enduring God knows what." He lifted his clear blue gaze to Dade. "We can't let an agency control our destiny like that anymore. At some point, we have to own what we are and make our stand. That time feels like now."

"Cody, you'll have the eyes of the whole damn world on us. On Aaron and Rory. On Ma and Gage's mate and cubs. Not just IESA. *The world.*"

"I've heard your piece," Cody said, his face stern as if he'd already made up his mind. "I'll talk to the crews we know and see what they think, but we can't let Shayna rebuild IESA. We can't wait around to be killed off when we don't do what they want."

Dade ran his hands through his hair and settled the frustrated rumble in his throat. "I'm out of here. I'll see you later."

"Later," Boone and Gage muttered in unison.

He strode out of the station, past the fire engine and the ambulance, and out into the cool evening air. Linking his hands behind his head, he stared up at the half moon. For some stupid reason he didn't understand, all he wanted to do right now was go see Quinn at the little cabin he'd followed her scent to earlier. *Quinn.* Just her name warmed him. Which didn't make any damned sense because he didn't even know the woman. And what he did know of her should've had him running in the opposite direction. She was mousy. An easy crier with a too-soft heart for his world. If she knew the things he'd done, she'd run and hide from what he was. She'd had trouble giving a dog a shot today. What chance did she have in his world?

None. She would be a casualty of what he was, especially if Cody was going to take the Breck Crew public.

What he needed was a good Lisa fuck to get Quinn off his mind, but when he thought of the woman he occasionally hooked up with, his dick deflated completely. This wasn't like him. The women he went out with knew the drill. No commitment, no attachment. Fun only and leave emotions at the door. Quinn had him all mixed up inside. Probably because she'd been all frail and needy. He'd always had a weak spot for vulnerable things. Tank included.

He couldn't talk to his brothers about Quinn or his inconvenient feelings for a stranger. They'd go straight to Ma and wouldn't ever let him live this down. But he felt crazy inside, all churning and volatile, as if his bear was going to rip out of him without warning. He'd always maintained perfect control over his animal—through two tours of service, through a dozen black ops missions, even when Krueger had hit that kill switch. But now, his beast was snarling to escape, and he didn't understand it. He was the brother who didn't feel. That was his gig, and it had served him well. In this life, survival depended on the ability to weather anything. He'd gone years without feeling a damned thing, and now some human was turning him into a half-crazed, protective-as-hell lunatic.

He sauntered to his pickup, slid behind the wheel and slammed the door beside him. Behind the wheel, he opened his phone and listened for the subtle clicking sound that would tell him if he was being monitored. Silence had him hitting speed dial for someone who might give him good advice. For someone who could settle him down and tell him to get ahold of himself and forget about Quinn in light of the shit storm that was about to barrel down on the Breck Crew.

The blare of guitar and a steady country song blasted through the phone a split second before Bruiser answered, "Hello?"

"Hey, man."

"Dade? Hang on." Bruiser's voice lowered as he said, "I'll be right back, D. It's my brother."

An involuntary smile took Dade's face. He'd never heard Bruiser call him family without specifying he was only his *half*-brother. Damn, he was glad Bruiser was back on speaking terms with the Breck Crew. The music faded in the background, but he winced as a blast of static wind hurt his sensitive ears.

"Sorry, man," Bruiser muttered. "We're out at Sammy's watching Denison and Brighton play a set."

"Oh, you want me to call you back later?"

"Nah, no reception up at the trailer park. Besides, it's good to hear your voice. How's things?"

Dade screwed up his face and traced the steering wheel with his fingertip. "Not awesome. Shayna is back."

"Shayna?"

"IESA agent. And she's come back begging a cub. Someone has Changed her, and she's agreed to be part of some reproductive research project Krueger was going after before...well...you know." Before Damon Daye ate his stupid ass.

"Shee-yit."

"Yep."

"What are you going to do?"

"Cody wants to go public. Take the power from IESA and out the agency along with us. It's a desperation move."

"Or it's time."

"Maybe. I don't know. Listen, I have a question I need to ask you. I can't bring it to Gage, Boone, or Cody because they'll go straight to Ma with it and—"

"Hey, how do you know I won't go to Ma with it?"

Dade frowned at the row of streetlights that lined the road in front of the station. "Are you and Ma talking again?"

"Yeah, but your secret is safe with me. Shoot when ready."

Wait, Bruiser was talking to Ma again? He was the half-dragon, half-bear result of an affair between his dad and Bruiser's mother. Ma hadn't found out about Bruiser until he was ten when Dad had died. She'd raised him to adulthood, but she'd struggled with it, and unfortunately, Bruiser had felt the chill of her inability to get over Dad's betrayal. If they were talking again, hell was probably starting to freeze over. "Damn, okay. Sorry, that just shocked me to my feet. You and Ma?"

Bruiser chuckled and said, "Yeah, my mate won't let me hold grudges on family. She's been good for my relationships."

Dade smiled, feeling better as his bear settled. "Dang, man, that's great. You don't even know how happy that makes me. We felt broken when you weren't talking to us. It just felt like something was missing, you know?"

"I know," he said quietly. "For me, too."

"Okay, I have a question about women."

"Women or a woman?"

"Maybe one woman. You know me, know how I operate. No commitment and all that."

"Mm-hmm."

Dade inhaled deeply and switched the phone to his other ear. "Look, I met this girl today when I took the station dog to the vet, and now she's filling my head, making me feel out of control. I hate it."

"But you don't hate her."

"She's soft, Bruiser. I mean, submissive, easily wounded. She's like a damned hummingbird." Beautiful with her soft auburn locks and wide, gray eyes. Fragile. Too delicate for a man like him to protect.

Bruiser chuckled into the speaker. "Did your bear perk up around her?"

"My bear and my dick. Which doesn't make a lick of sense because she was crying the whole time I was with her. What kind of man gets a boner around a sobbing woman?"

"She pulled at your heartstrings?"

"Every damned one of them. I can't stop thinking about her. How do I turn this off?"

"You don't, brother. You dig your heels in and get ready. Your bear just chose his mate. Good luck trying to forget her."

Dade's mouth dropped open, and he clacked his mouth closed again. "That's it? I've chosen and I'm done for?"

"Not done for, Dade. You're lucky. If your bear chose her, then she's a good match for you."

"Yeah, well the timing couldn't be worse. Shayna's after me, tailing me, and I can't have Quinn in her sites. And the bigger problem is that Cody is about to take us public. I can't drag her through that. She wouldn't survive it."

"Maybe she's stronger than you think," Bruiser said in a soft, thoughtful tone. "You chose her for a reason."

"I thought you didn't believe in fate."

"Yeah, then I married my mate sight unseen, and she's it for me. She came into my life at just the right moment to set everything right again. Trust your animal. Trust your instincts."

"I'll hurt her."

"Maybe. Maybe not."

Dade shook his head in denial. He'd planned on going his whole life just as he had been. Fucking occasionally to settle his animal, then going about his business. He liked things the way they were. His personal life was simple and easy. He didn't have to worry about anyone besides himself and his crew. Cody had become scared when his mate Rory brought their young son to him, begging help with his little out-of-control bear. That had to be why Cody was making a desperate decision now. Pairing up with a mate changed things, made men softer, weaker. He didn't want that. He'd spent a lifetime erecting walls of stone and mortar around his heart out of necessity. He wasn't going to live forever, or even much longer in trigger-happy IESA's crosshairs, and now his bear had latched onto a helpless human.

"You know, you were supposed to be the level-headed one," Dade muttered.

"I am. You just don't like hearing what I have to say. But hey, have fun trying to stay away from your mate." His voice was practically singing.

Dade leaned his head back on the chair. "This sucks. Does it get better with time?"

"If you're talking about thinking about her constantly, it gets worse over time."

"But not if I don't talk to her again. My bear will eventually give up on her."

A beat of silence. "You can try, man. I know the timing doesn't feel right, but there is a reason she came into your life right now."

Dade talked to him for a few minutes longer, then hung up, more confused than when he'd called. Bruiser was supposed to have told him how to break away from whatever spell Quinn had cast on him. She couldn't be worse for him, or he for her. Oil and water.

If she had any shot at happiness, it wasn't with him.

He was a meteor on a collision course with the human race.

If he pulled her along for the ride, she'd burn up right along with him.

FOUR

When the bacon grease in the skillet popped, Quinn yanked her hand back. She glared at a tiny dot of moisture that burned on the knuckle of her thumb. Today hadn't been awesome. Confusing, irritating, and heart wrenching, yes, but awesome, absolutely not.

Daffodil huffed a yip from beside her, and she frowned at the tiny Yorkshire Terrier. Daffodil wasn't a barker by nature. She was more of a lazy, eat while lying next to the food bowl, sleep through a burglary type of dog. The exact opposite of her breed traits. It was Beans that had been the barker in his younger days, but now her senior yorkie just lounged around the oversize bed she had set up for him in the corner of the kitchen. Old as a dinosaur, deaf and nearly blind, he wasn't the best watch dog either.

The fact that Daffodil had barked set off clanging warning alarms in Quinn's head. She turned off the knob to the stovetop and padded toward the window. Her eyes flew wide and she guffawed when she saw Dade's jacked-up Tacoma sitting on the street at the end of her long, gravel driveway. How the hell did he know where she lived?

She pulled back the curtain a little farther with the tip of her finger as he strode up the stone walkway, only to turn around and jog back to his truck. A curse word echoed through the window as he ran his hands through his blond hair. Short on the sides and longer up top, it was sticking up everywhere as if he'd roughed it up a few times already.

He turned and glared over his shoulder at her front door. His angry expression confused her. What had she done? Answer: not a darn thing. He was the one who had been hot and cold at the vet's office, then sprayed travel grit in her face as he drove away.

Dade hooked his hands on his hips and stared off into the woods across the road.

Okaaay...right here was a man completely at war with himself, but why?

He spun and strode for her front door, then stopped halfway and stomped back toward his pickup again. When he opened his door, it became apparent he was really leaving this time, and a piece of her revolted at not finding out what he wanted.

In a rush, she pulled a few pieces of bacon from the skillet and wrapped them in a paper towel, then bolted for the door just as the engine roared to life.

"Wait!" she called, sprinting for his truck, the hem of her robe flapping behind her. It wasn't until she reached his Tacoma that the chill on her legs reminded her she hadn't checked her clothes before she left the house.

"Oh, crap," she said on a breath as she looked down in horror at her bare legs.

Dade opened the door with a look akin to amusement on his face where she'd expected anger. "What are you wearing?"

She opened her mouth and snapped it closed again, unable to hold his gaze for more than a second. "I brought you bacon."

The smile dipped from his face, and the corners

of his eyes tightened. "Bacon?"

"Boys like bacon," she rushed out, regretting the words as they tumbled past her lips.

Dade scratched his ear and scanned the street behind him. "You don't have any pants on."

Grimacing, she handed him the wrapped meat and pulled her robe around her. "Sorry."

"I don't mind at all," he said, eyebrows arching high. "You look fuckin' hot." Dade cleared his throat and stared at her bare feet. His contrite expression said he deeply regretted those words.

"I'm making breakfast for dinner. You want to come in?" she asked.

"Best if I don't." He held up the tiny, greasy care package. "Thanks for the bacon." His eyes dropped to her silky robe once more before he got into his truck and shut the door.

"Bye," she murmured in confusion as he sped away from her for the second time in one day.

Down the street, a pair of headlights turned on, and a black sedan coasted by. It looked like the one from earlier. The windows were tinted, which made it impossible to see inside, but the car brought gooseflesh to Quinn's arms, and she pulled the robe tighter around her frame.

Cop shows were her favorite guilty pleasure. She didn't know what Dade was into, but he was definitely being followed.

****

One week had passed, and Dade had disappeared like he'd never existed at all. Impressive since this was a small town, and she'd looked for him everywhere she went. Not on purpose, but her heart seemed hell-bent on getting another glimpse of the handsome mystery man who couldn't be polite for more than thirty seconds. What did that say about her? That she was interested in a man who's communication skills were horrid.

He was nothing like Jay.

The thought of him slashed pain through her middle, but the flood gates had opened now, and as she refilled shelves of medicine in the back room, she couldn't help the memories that washed over her. Everything had been easy with Jay. Natural and simple. She'd met him when she was fourteen, and they'd grown up together. She'd planned on forever, but forever hadn't lasted much longer than his nineteenth birthday.

She'd been perfectly content to stay single for the rest of her life, protecting her heart from that kind of pain again, but Dade had come in and stirred up feelings she hadn't felt in a long time, like a flood kicking up silt from a river bottom.

Oh, she knew he was dangerous. The scar on his neck said he'd been through something awful and survived. And his cold demeanor was one he'd learned. Callousness like that didn't come from leading an easy life. And then there was the black sedan watching his every move. Perhaps it was a bodyguard, keeping him safe from something, but what on God's green and blue planet could threaten a behemoth of a man like Dade? He seemed so sure of himself, invincible even.

She imagined not much scared a man like him.

But intrigued by his backstory or not, he obviously wasn't interested in her. For the hundredth time, she kicked herself for that stupid bacon line she'd used on him. *Boys like bacon.* Good grief. She was terrible at flirting. In her defense though, she hadn't dated anyone since Jay. Six years, and the man she'd decided to latch onto was clearly unavailable and equally disinterested. Her flirting skills were about as rusty as a nail a decade under water.

Not to mention he was seven levels out of her league! Quinn glared in the mirror above a small sink in the corner. She'd been wearing extra make-up everyday on the off chance he would swing by. All that effort wasted on a ghost.

"Quinn?" Dr. Voss asked, sticking her head through the doorway. "I'm headed out. Are you almost finished with inventory?"

"Oh, yeah. I'll have it done in half an hour, tops. I can lock up if you want me to."

"That would be great. My daughter has a recital tonight, and I need to get home and change before it starts."

"Yeah, no worries. I'll see you tomorrow. Have fun at the recital."

Dr. Voss smiled and nodded. "I will. You have a good night, too."

Quinn smiled as the vet left. She liked her. Dr. Voss was only a few years older, but she had a calm maturity that Quinn admired. No matter what kind of trauma came through the front doors, Dr. Voss always handled it with grace and poise and always knew just what to say to a family grieving a pet. And she'd been kind enough not to have Quinn assist on any more pet euthanasia, bless that woman. Gertie didn't seem to have any trouble with it, for which Quinn was eternally grateful.

A pair of tabby cats that had been spayed mewed at her from the cages along the wall. Unable to resist them as they rubbed themselves down the sides of the wire cages, she strode over and pet them until they were purring in contented waves. The ding of the bell on the front door was quiet but distinct from the back room. It must be Dr. Voss, back because she forgot something.

But when the veterinarian didn't come to the back room, Quinn began to worry it was a customer, come late with an emergency. "Hang on," she called out, weaving around the boxes of medicine stacked willy nilly on the floor. "I'm coming!"

When she reached for the door handle, the click of metal on metal sounded. The tiny noise chilled her blood, and she pulled hard. The door didn't budge.

"Hello? Is someone out there?" Her voice sounded much higher than she'd intended.

Jamming her foot against the wall, she gripped the handle again and pulled with all her strength.

Nothing. "What the heck?"

She jogged for the back exit, then yanked on the knob. That one was stuck, too. Shoot. Jerking over and over with all of her might proved to be fruitless. Panic sent her heart rate to skittering against her ribs as she searched the room for something to pry open the door. Nah, forget that. She was calling the police. Someone had locked her in here on purpose. She didn't know why, but she needed help.

Shaking, clammy hands made her drop the cell as soon as she dug it out of her back pocket, but thankfully, it still worked. She dialed 911 and told the automated message system the address. A local operator picked up.

"Someone has locked me inside of the Tiny Paws Vet clinic off of Main. I'm in a back room and need help. I can't get either of the exit doors open."

"All right," an elderly sounding woman said. "Just remain calm. I'm sending someone to you right now."

Something pungent and thick hit her nose, and she clutched the cell phone tighter.

"Ma'am?" she asked, voice shaking.

"Yes, dear?"

"I smell smoke."

FIVE

Dade lay back on his bed in the single room he'd been assigned to at the station. Linking his hands behind his head, he stared up at the tiles in the ceiling and tried for the billionth time to ignore the urge to beg a grocery run with the guys just to drive by the veterinary clinic and see if Quinn's bike was out front.

Whatever the woman had done to him, it sucked. Holding any kind of focus was a joke, and now he'd lost his appetite. And worst of all, his inner grizzly was more restless than one of those caged bears at the zoo. He winced as his stomach turned again. He'd Changed four times this week, and still, he felt barely in control of his own skin.

He'd just got done with a shower after a two

hour heavy-weight workout, and still he couldn't get his mind off her. He thought if he refused to see her, his bear would give up, but the mean old cuss was just getting more and more pissed as each day passed.

Maybe Bruiser had been right. Maybe he should trust his instincts.

The alarm sounded, and he lurched up. The dispatcher came over the loudspeaker, announced a fire in progress, and recited the address. She called up the paramedics, too, and said a woman was trapped.

Fuck, he hated these. Every second counted when there was a life in the grip of those flames. Adrenaline pumped through his bloodstream as he sprinted down the hall and out to the hanger where the engine sat ready. Already, Boone and Gage were donning their gear as Cody, dressed and ready, barked out orders into a radio at his shoulder.

The address was right off Main Street, down at the end and near a wooded area, so there was a risk of igniting the dry pine needle floor around the building. He skidded to a stop near his turnout gear. He'd dressed for fires so many times he could do it without thinking. Stepped into the trousers, into the boots, pulled up the suspenders and latched them in place. Pulled on the jacket, button, button, button. Velcroed the neck. Helmet on and oxygen tank flipped over his head and on like a backpack, clicked into place at his waist and tightened to secure it. He grabbed his mask and gloves and bolted for the engine. Now he was waterproof, heat proof, and ready to hop up into big old red clanging Engine 4.

He jumped in the back seat with Gage while Boone took shotgun and Cody drove. His alpha was fire chief of this station, and Boone had just been promoted to captain a few months back. Above, he could hear the other three crew members settling on top of the engine. Clutching the grab bar, Dade looked back to make sure the ambulance was following. Lights flashing, sirens blaring, Cody blasted down Main Street.

Dade's heart was already pounding, but the closer they got to the vet clinic, the more the fine hairs on his arms raised, even in the stifling heat of his turnout gear.

"Hey, what was that address again?" he asked.

Cody recited it, but it didn't ring a bell. He didn't

know the exact address of the clinic. But as they turned off the main road and he saw the black plumes of smoke, he jolted upright.

"No, no, no!" he yelled, lurching out of the engine before it had stopped. "Quinn!"

"Who's Quinn?" Boone called.

No time to explain, Dade ran ignored him and sprinted toward the back of the clinic.

Two men were trying frantically to pry something off the door handle.

"Dade," Cody called out over the radio on his shoulder. "Stand down. We need to assess this before you go in there. Repeat, stand down."

"She's mine, Cody," he gasped out, choking on the smog. He pulled his mask on as Boone muttered a curse from right behind him. Everything was different once his mask was securely over his face. Sound changed, became muffled, and smell was all but nothing. Pulling on his gloves, he yelled Quinn's name again as he pushed past the two men trying to open the door. Every window around the side was engulfed in flames.

Please, God, let it not be too late.

A metal pipe had been twisted around the

emergency exit, and the thing screeched as he pulled it apart. Fuck showing off his strength to the bystander humans right now. Dade didn't care about anything but getting to her.

Sweat dripped down the sides of his face as he growled and bent the pipe with all of his strength. With an echoing metal clang, it broke in his hands, and he tossed it to the side. Boone's hand was on his back, and Cody was murmuring a string of orders through the radio Dade couldn't make out over the roaring in his ears.

Please let there not be a backdraft.

It was then that he heard it. Pained screams from the woman he'd been dreaming about. Throwing open the door, he ran through the fire-rimmed frame.

"Fire department, call out!" he yelled.

The smoke was so thick he couldn't see. He'd never been in this room, so he had no guess how big it was or where Quinn could be. Smoke billowed through the open door behind him as Boone stepped through.

"Fire Department. Quinn, call out!" he yelled again.

His brother pointed, and Dade's eyes adjusted to

the dim light.

Quinn wasn't screaming anymore, and she lay under a metal beam from the ceiling. With a sound of agony lodged in his throat, Dade bullied his way past burning boxes. Two cats rushed past his legs, headed for the door. She must've let them out of those open cages on the wall, hoping they would get out somehow.

"Help me!" he yelled, pointing to the hot metal over her legs. Boone and Gage took the other end and lifted. When it was off her by inches, Dade slid her out from under the rubble. No time to C-Collar her, he scooped her up as flames licked at her shoes. Boone kicked a path through the debris, but when they reached the door, the wall collapsed with a tremendous crash, blocking them in.

The powerhouse *whoosh* of hose water sounded against the walls, blasting holes too small to fit through.

Dade crouched and covered Quinn's body with his own. Gage was already going at another wall with an ax as he spoke to Cody through the radio.

Heat everywhere.

Burning.

Searing.

Even through his fire proof clothes, it was an inferno.

Smoke everywhere, covering everything, blocking the sun as he stumbled through the flaming wreckage.

Boone grabbed his jacket and pulled him through the opening Cody was cutting from the outside.

Running, panting, his breath so loud in the mask. Quinn's face was white as a sheet.

Dropping to his knees, Dade set her in the grass and yanked off his mask. She smelled like ash and death. He leaned over and checked her breathing. Shallow air was raggedly passing her lips, and her lungs made a rasping sound.

"Stay with me, Quinn," he demanded, yanking the C-Collar from Boone's hands. "Medic!" Where the fuck were they?

One glance at her legs, and a sound of devastation wrenched from his throat. Her jeans had been burned away across both thighs, leaving the skin underneath raw and open. And that's just what he saw on the outside. She could've broken her back or had internal bleeding.

Cody took off his mask and knelt down with a curse.

"I can fix this," Dade said on a desperate breath.

With his teeth, he bit his gloves and yanked them off. He lifted her arm in his hands.

"What are you doing?" Cody asked low.

"Changing her. She'll heal."

"Are you crazy? She'll Change instantly in front of everyone."

"I don't give a shit, Cody! That's what you wanted anyway, to out us." His voice dipped to a ragged whisper. "Please. She's my mate. Shayna did this to her because of me."

Cody's eyes looked horrified through the streaks of soot on his face. "Shayna? But why?"

"I need to get to her," a paramedic named Greg said, shoving his way through.

"Wait." Cody slashed his hand through the air, stopping Greg in his tracks. His brought his gaze back to Dade. "She's really yours? And she knows?"

Dade shook his head. "I pushed her away."

"Fuck, Dade! You can't Change her without her permission. No. She'll have to survive this on her own. Human."

Dade looked down at her legs, burned to the bone from that metal beam. Moisture blurred his vision. "I can't lose her. I'm sorry, Cody." Before his alpha could stop him, Dade sank his teeth into Quinn's arm and bit down until he could taste the iron in her blood.

"What are you doing?" Greg screamed. "Get away from her." He shoved Dade backward, but it was already too late.

Quinn's back bowed, and she made a choking sound.

Somberly, Dade removed his helmet and jacket.

Boone looked up at him from his place beside Quinn's seizing body. He shook his head and muttered, "Shhhit," then stood and removed his jacket, too.

A crowd was forming near the second fire engine that had been called in from Station 7. They joined the other half of their crew, working tirelessly with the hoses to calm the flames that engulfed the building.

Gage rolled his eyes closed, shook his head, and dropped his mask on the grass. "Well, no one will ever accuse us of not knowing how to make an entrance."

Cody cracked his neck and pointed to a teenager in the crowd who was taking video with his cell phone. "You might want to point that thing over here. We're about to make you famous online, kid."

A long snarl rattled Quinn's throat as her back arched against the ground again. Hands clenched, she screamed in the final moments before a red-furred grizzly ripped out of her skin.

The crowd surged backward, terrified cries filling the air as Quinn struggled to all fours. Her back legs weren't working, and her pupils were dilated with shock. Maybe this wouldn't work. Maybe she was too broken for a bear to fix her.

It was too late to regret his decision now because there was no turning back. Cody looked furious as he shrugged out of his turnout gear. Dade yanked his suspenders from his shoulders and pulled his shirt over his head just as Quinn lunged upward, wild abandon in her scared gaze. His bear exploded from him, shredding the top of his trousers on the way out. He roared a welcome as towering grizzlies burst from his brothers, one by one.

Most of the crowd was on the lam, but a few brave souls stayed around to take video and pictures. Some of the firefighters from their crew abandoned the hose to get away from them, leaving Station 7 to take the brunt of the flames.

Dade slammed down onto all fours in front of her as Quinn tried to charge the crowd. From the vacant look in her eyes, she didn't have her mind, and Dade would be damned if he Changed her, then allowed her to do something she would regret for all time. If she struggled to put an ailing dog to sleep, she'd be destroyed if she hurt someone now.

Fury in her eyes, she attacked Dade, clawing and biting, but he was helpless to defend himself against her. He wouldn't hurt her worse than she was by raking a warning claw down her flesh. Cody stood on all fours and bellowed a roar so loud, Quinn hunched down in front of him. He narrowed blazing eyes at her, gold as fire against his dark fur. When he took a thundering step forward, Quinn fell back on her injured legs. The acrid smell of her fear pulled a warning growl from Dade's throat, but Cody wasn't backing down.

Quinn was beautiful—wide, churning green-gold

eyes, dark nose set against auburn fur that shone like sparks in the sunlight. A soft, confused noise rattled her chest as she froze. With a sharp inhalation, she sank back into her human skin.

"They'll kill her," a woman screamed from the crowd.

Metal cracked on metal, and Dade threw himself over Quinn's crumpled body just as the first shot rang out. Pain blasted through his shoulder.

Cody was yelling now, and Dade looked over his shoulder to see him back in his human form, holding his jacket in front of his dick and trying to calm the crowd.

"He won't hurt her. She's his mate. He's just trying to protect her. Please, put the weapons down so I can get my crew to Change back. They won't hurt you. You have my word."

"The word of a monster!" a man clutching a handgun shouted from the edge of the growing masses.

"We aren't monsters. We're citizens just like you, and we don't hurt humans. Please, my brother is just trying to save his girl. Greg! Can you help her? She needs to go to the hospital. Her legs are badly burned."

"What are you?" a woman asked from her hiding place, peeking around the fire engine.

"We're bear shifters. Very rare. Greg. Please, man, she needs help."

Greg stepped cautiously from beside the ambulance. "You bit her. Why?"

"Don't answer any more questions," a blond-haired woman ordered from the crowd. "I think you should think carefully about the things that come from your mouth right now. An informal interview will only hurt you when emotions are running high like this. Plus, your brother has been shot."

"Who are you?" Cody asked.

"I work for the news. I'll break this story if you want me to, but I think we need to take a step back."

The woman's voice rang with honesty, and her hazel eyes swam with concern.

"Okay, no more," Cody conceded.

"Will she turn into that thing again?" Greg asked, approaching with his med kit slowly.

"Not now," Cody said. "Not for another week at least. Look at her." He jerked his head toward Quinn's limp body lying between Dade's front paws. "She's half dead."

"I'm not working on her with three grizzlies looking over my shoulder. You're the leader, right? Get them to turn into humans again so I don't have to worry about my life while I'm trying to save hers."

"Change back." Cody's voice cracked with authority, and Dade's body caved in on itself.

Growling at the pain of his forced Change, coupled with the seeping bullet wound that was burning his shoulder from the inside out, he was barely able to keep the scream in his throat as he melted into his human skin again. Exhausted, he slid into what was left of his trousers and hoped his dick wasn't hanging out for the news crew that had just pulled up.

He watched, anguished, as Greg and other paramedics that had been called to the scene, worked over Quinn. Her eyes were open, staring vacantly at the sky as her body was jostled and moved, and Dade fell to his knees as Greg placed an oxygen mask on her.

"Her lungs are struggling from the smoke inhalation." Greg's voice drifted in and out of Dade's consciousness. "...Burns... blood transfusion... both legs... broken... internal bleeding..."

He hadn't saved her at all. The bear inside of her was strong and would give her the ability to heal faster, but some things were too bad to fix instantly. He knew that. The scars on his torso and neck were proof of shifter mortality. The smell of her burned flesh was further proof that saving her hadn't been as simple as a bite from him.

And now Quinn, his Quinn, was hurt badly. If she lived, she'd be scarred for always, just like him.

He'd done this.

Poisoned her life with his presence.

That man in the crowd was right.

Dade wiped Quinn's blood from his mouth with the back of his hand.

He was a monster.

SIX

The *beep beep beeping* of a machine pulled Quinn from the deep folds of sleep. Her throat was dry, and when she tried to open her eyes, something kept her from being able to do so. Reaching up, she felt around her face. Tape adhered her lids together, and in a moment of panic, she pulled at the corners and yanked them off.

Her vision was blurry, so she blinked rapidly until it cleared. She was in a hospital room with a large viewing window. Outside, she could see two uniformed police officers. She ripped out the tube pushing oxygen into her nose and tugged at the IV in her arm. The beeping flat lined as she ridded herself of the plethora of wires and contraptions attached to her body.

Fumbling, she pushed the red button on her bed. "Hello?"

A doctor bustled in, and both cops rested their hands on their guns as they watched her through the window.

"Where am I?" she asked, voice sounding like she'd swallowed glass and gravel.

"You're at St. Anthony's. Shhh, please, Quinn. You have to stay calm, or they won't let me stay in here with you."

"What do you mean? I don't understand. Why am I here?"

The doctor's blond ponytail swished as she froze. Her blue eyes went round with shock. "Don't you remember what happened to you?"

Quinn rubbed her head and tried to recall the time before she'd been in here. Flashes of memories assaulted her. Gravel, black sedan, two cats, Dade...*Dade*. Work, inventory, flames...

She gasped as it came back to her. Horrified, she pulled the sheets back to reveal her bandaged legs. "I want to see them."

"I don't think that's a good idea."

Quinn read the doctor's nametag. "Moira, please."

"Swear not to hurt me if I take the bandages off?"

"Hurt you? Why would I hurt you?"

Her delicate eyebrows drew down. "What is the last thing you remember?"

"Burning."

"Nothing more?"

Quinn squinted her eyes, trying to dredge up anything more, but there was simply nothing there. "Fire, pain, then here."

Moira leaned over the bed and pressed an intercom button. "Call him," was all she said.

Static sounded, and a feminine voice came over the other line. "But Lieutenant Danvers said—"

"Call him," Moira said sternly.

"Call who?" Quinn asked low.

"Someone who can explain what happened to you much better than I can. You ready to see?"

Quinn swallowed the coward down and nodded.

It hurt. Holy hell it was agony to take the bandages off, but Moira didn't slow down or give her time to back out. And when Quinn laid her eyes on her scarred legs, a piece of her broke. Across her thighs, her skin had melted, and now resembled red Oklahoma clay.

"How long have I been out?"

"Two days."

Quinn jerked her attention to Moira's face. Her voice sounded clear as a bell. She didn't know how she could tell, but Moira was telling the truth.

"Two days?" Quinn dragged her shocked gaze back down to her legs. "But these look half healed."

"They are. You might have some muscle weakness, and possibly a limp, but you'll make almost a full recovery."

"And the scars?"

Moira shook her head sadly.

Quinn leaned back against the pillow and stared at the sterile ceiling. "When can I go home?"

"I don't know."

"But you're a doctor. Surely, you can tell how long it will take me to heal."

Moira looked pointedly at the officers outside. "It's not up to me or any of the medical staff here, Quinn. It's up to the government."

"What?" she asked on a breath. "What does the government have to do with me? I pay my taxes." She twitched her head at an escalating noise outside. "I don't even have a speeding ticket on my record." The noise grew louder, pricking her ears until they tingled. "What is that?"

"What's what?"

"That noise. People. A crowd…jeering." She lurched out of bed and hissed at the searing pain that blasted up her legs. With a groan of shock, she used the chair to steady herself, then shuffled over to the window. The gown she wore was backless, and she was giving Moira quite the show of her ass, but right now, she didn't care so much about that. Below, thousands of people had gathered. Some held signs, but she could only read one from here.

Cage the Animals.

Animals?

A black SUV pulled through the crowd slowly, and when the door opened, she perked up. Dade and another blond-haired man filed out and made their way slowly through the crowd. The masses surged forward, clawing and touching them. Dade lifted his feral gaze, golden green, up to her window and held her frozen fast.

"What's wrong with him?" she asked.

Moira inhaled deeply. "As far as I'm concerned, nothing is wrong with him. You either."

Frowning, Quinn twisted. "Why has Dade come to see me?"

"Because Dade Keller is the reason you are here."

Confusion washed over her, making it hard for her to breath. Indeed, he'd felt dangerous the first time she'd met him, and cold when he'd sped away from her on the street. "Dade set the fire?"

"No. Dade isn't the one who put you here in this hospital, Quinn. He is the reason you're still alive." Moira stood and smoothed the wrinkles from her lavender scrubs. "You have about five minutes before he reaches this room." She twitched her head toward the bathroom and smiled. "Push the button if you need me."

Leaning heavily on the chair, then the bed, Quinn made her way to the bathroom and guffawed when she saw her pallid reflection in the mirror. She looked like an unwashed, unkempt vampire. With a growl, she sponged off in the shower, careful not to get her burns wet. Shaving her legs with the disposable razor on the lip of the shower sounded like hell, so she settled for shampooing her hair while bent forward under the water. Teeth brushed, face washed, and cheeks pinched, she shuffled out the door and froze. Dade sat on her rumpled hospital bed, shirt off and long, deep scars on his back exposed. Moira was checking something under a bandage across his shoulder. Eyes still blazing that feral color, he slid her a glance over his shoulder, then pulled his T-shirt back over his scarred body.

"It looks fine," Moira said. "Who took the bullet out?"

Dade nodded to a man in the corner. "My brother, Boone, did."

"With what?" Moira asked.

"With my finger," Boone said with an empty smile.

"Truth," Quinn whispered. "You're telling the truth."

The brothers each shot the other a loaded look.

"But how do I know that?" she asked low.

Boone pushed off the wall, his blue eyes troubled as he twitched his head. His shoulder-length blond hair flicked out from in front of his face, and he stuck his oversize hand out for a shake. Up one arm, he was completely covered with a full sleeve of tattoos. "I'm

Boone Keller. You probably don't remember me, but I was there when you came to be, little bear."

"Little bear," she repeated softly, shaking his hand.

His words tugged at the frayed end of a memory she'd buried deeply.

"Right. Well, I'm going to leave you to it." He jerked his chin toward the officers by the window. "I'll be outside."

Dade sat on the bed, his profile to her, watching her warily from the corner of his eye. "I have something to say, and I suck with words, so just let me say it and get it done."

She shuffled toward the bed, but the pain in her legs made her wince and lose her balance. "Shhhoot," she hissed, leaning heavily, arms locked against the mattress.

A growling sound came from behind her, and when she took stock of her body, Dade's hands were gripping her waist, steadying her from behind. How the heck had he ended up over here?

She narrowed her eyes at her splayed hands, in instincts screaming not to keep him at her back. "What are you?"

"Well, that's part of what I want to talk to you about. I'm a shifter."

"Meaning?"

"I turn into a bear when I want. Or lately when I'm worked up."

She snorted and sank heavily onto the mattress. Sure, it sounded like he was being honest from the clear bell tone of his voice, but he wasn't a bear. "Okay, Dade Keller, where'd you get all those scars on your back?"

"I did two tours. Shrapnel."

The smile fell from her lips as her humor faded away. "Are you still active duty?"

He shook his head and sat beside her. "Let me see your legs."

"Why, because the open back of my hospital gown wasn't enough? You'll have to buy me dinner before I show you my gorgeous gams." She'd meant it as a joke, but her voice had faded and hitched by the last word. Her heart pounded around Dade, and she had the fluttering of emotions she hadn't felt in years when she looked into his eyes. Nothing in her wanted to show him how messed up her body was now.

"I didn't look at the back of your gown."

"Because you didn't want to?" The answer mattered.

Dade canted his head and blinked once, slowly. "I wanted to look, but I didn't think you would be comfortable with it."

She took a relieved breath and brushed her fingertips across the melted skin on his neck. "And this?"

Dade gripped her wrist and pushed it away. His Adam's apple bobbed as he swallowed and gave her a hard look. "I've given you enough for now."

Him flinching away from her touch ripped at her heart. "Why don't you like for me to touch you?"

"Because," he whispered, "I haven't earned it."

"Moira said you saved my life."

"Moira was mistaken. I was the one who ruined your life. You just haven't realized it yet."

"Did you pull me from the fire?"

A single nod.

"Why were you there?"

"Because it was my job."

She could decipher the wavering note in his words enough to know that wasn't the whole truth. She pulled her shoulders up to her ears and scrunched up her nose. "Honestly?"

"Fuck," he muttered, looking out the window as he released her wrist. "I'm a firefighter. I was at the station when the call came through."

"Were you scared, running into those flames?"

"No. I was scared that when I came out with you, you'd already be gone."

Truth.

Her heart thumped erratically against her breastbone. "Why do you care? You don't even know me."

Dade lifted one shoulder in a miserable half-shrug and rubbed his hand down his short blond stubble. It made a scratching sound against his palm. She stared at his facial hair, shining gold in the sunlight that streamed through the window. She wanted badly to touch, just to see if it was as soft as it looked. His eyes were still bright but had lost that muddy, wild color. "I care about what happens to you. I care if you're safe. I care if you're happy."

"But why? What have I done to earn that? I thought you disliked me."

"What?"

"You sped off and sprayed me with gravel

instead of offering me a ride when my bike tire was flat, Dade. That's the least romantic thing I've ever encountered, and it happened to me."

He grimaced and rolled his bandaged shoulder. "Look, I know it's a lot to take in, and I promise I'll tell you everything, but I'd rather do it in private."

She made a show of looking around. "There's no one here but you and me."

Dade stared at her long and hard. "Boone can hear us clear as day, just like you could hear the officers talking across the hall if you chose to listen. There's a security camera in that corner and another over there." He pointed, and sure enough, there were. "Not to mention, the room is likely bugged."

"Okay, you're scaring me."

"I won't let anything happen to you. I promise."

"Then why did you say you ruined my life? And why am I in a hospital room guarded by cops and mobbed by a crowd holding *Cage the Animals* signs?" Her voice wrenched up to a Level Shrill, but she was in it now—full blown panic mode and gaining speed like a boulder down a mountainside.

"Quinn," Dade warned low, holding his hands out. "You have to stay calm."

"Why does everyone keep saying that? I'm a buck twenty-five with flimsy arms. I've never hurt anyone in my life. Why is everyone walking on eggshells every time I ask serious questions? Who locked me in that room, Dade? I heard someone come in. Who set that fire? I want to know everything." Her vision blurred with unshed tears, and she blinked them back, determined not to show him how weak she felt. "Who gave me these?" She yanked her hospital gown up around her thighs, exposing the burns that stung relentlessly with a bone-deep, throbbing ache.

Dade reared back as if he'd been slapped. He stood, then retreated a few steps away from her. A muscle in his jaw twitched as he linked his hands behind his head and let off a helpless sound.

"Who, Dade?"

"Me, all right? You have those because of me."

Horror congealed in her veins, making it hard to move. "You set the fire? You locked me in that room?"

"No, but I might as well have. If I'd have just stayed away from you, Shayna would've left you alone. You would've never been on her radar, but I put you right in her path." Dade's eyes filled with emotion as he swallowed hard and looked ill. "Shayna locked you in that room and set the fire, but it wasn't for you, Quinn. She was trying to get to me."

"But...you don't know me. Why would this Shayna woman go after me if I'm a stranger to you?"

"Because you're mine." The words came out gritty and low, almost too quiet for her to make them out.

"What?"

"Because my animal chose you. Because I want you. Because I can't see anything but you."

"But you peeled out and threw gravel in my face!" None of this made any sense. He didn't like her. He struggled to even be nice to her.

"I was trying to throw Shayna off your trail. She was tailing me, and I wanted her to think you didn't mean anything to me, but she went after you anyway. It was a dick move, leaving you on the side of the road like that—"

"This isn't how picking someone works! You haven't even kissed me! How do you know I'm yours when you haven't even kissed me?"

Dade rushed to her and cupped her neck. Hesitating only a moment, he leaned down and pressed his lips onto hers.

Quinn gripped his shirt and pushed him, her instincts poised to claw him—for the unexpected kiss and everything he'd just admitted. But Dade didn't give an inch. Instead, he cupped her other cheek and angled his head, then licked the closed seam of her lips, melting her completely.

Flutters started at her toes and worked their way into her stomach as she gripped onto his wrists to keep his hands there. She was safe like this, with him. Dade was big and strong. He'd pulled her from the burning building and had come right away so she wouldn't be all alone here in this hospital. And this big, tough, scarred up man had just admitted to feelings for her—deep ones. The kind that she'd been missing for so long. The kind she'd wanted from him. As much as she tried to convince herself he was dangerous to her heart, Dade was what she'd yearned for. Since he'd come into the vet clinic and been tender with her tears, she'd been enamored by him, despite his moments of confounding aloofness. She'd stayed up nights thinking about him, and her heart pounded every time someone entered the vet's office on the off-chance that it would be him. Silly? Sure.

She was acting like a school girl with a crush, but she couldn't help it. This man intrigued her in ways that were utterly baffling and exciting at the same time.

With a soft gasp, she opened her mouth and let him taste her. His jaw worked as he maneuvered in between her spread thighs and leaned his body closer. His warmth seeped into her, and she cuddled closer, desperate to forget everything that had happened, even if it was just for a little while.

Dade's hand gripped her ribs, arched her toward him until she sat on the very edge of the bed. A soft groan of want escaped her lips. His breath shook as he eased back and plucked at her lips once. Twice. Leaving her with delicious little smacks until, at last, he rested his forehead against hers and closed his eyes. She understood. She was savoring him, too.

"Wow," she murmured, leaning her cheek against his palm and feeling utterly drunk.

His sensual lips turned up in a sad smile. "I'm sorry, Quinn."

Confused, she frowned and eased back. "Sorry for what?"

"For this." He brushed his fingertips down her arm and pulled her wrist until the underside of her forearm was exposed. A faded, pink scar in the perfect shape of teeth marks decorated her pale skin, just inside her elbow.

"Is that a..."

He nodded, failing to meet her eyes. Leaning down, he kissed the scar gently, then rubbed the pad of his thumb across the raised mark.

"Why did you do that?"

He winced at the accusation in her tone, but hang it all. This morning, she'd been happy. She'd known exactly how her day was going to go, and now, because of Dade, she was hurt and scarred and in trouble with the government, and this was all too much.

"I did it because I thought it would save you. It's a claiming mark."

"And a claiming mark means I'm yours?" Anger blasted through her chest as she clutched wads of her hospital gown in her fists. He'd done something to her that meant a lot more than she was ready for, and without her consent. She crossed her arms over her chest and bit her lip hard to stop the tremble there. "I want to go home."

He looked sick as he nodded slowly.

"Please," she begged in a ragged whisper.

"Okay, Quinn. I'll see what I can do."

SEVEN

Quinn sat there wide-eyed with her lips pursed as she listened to Dade ream out the police guards who seemed determined to keep her here. She could both see them through the window and hear them clear as day.

"We aren't under arrest, are we? No? Then we're going."

"We have strict orders to keep her here until we hear otherwise."

"For what? She isn't some lab rat. She's a person, just like you. I'll write down the address where we will be staying, and you can follow us there and watch over us until you realize how fucking boring that job is since we're just people who get up every day and go to work. Just like you."

"Monroe," Boone's softer voice sounded. "You know us. Have known us for years. Have we ever hurt anyone?"

"No, man, and I hate this, too. You've only helped people that I've seen. I've watched you Kellers run back into burning buildings just to make sure they were clear and that everyone survived. Do I think this is right?" The dark-headed man shook his head. "But I have orders."

"She can't finish healing here, Monroe. She needs to be with her crew where we can take care of her. Adjusting to what she is in a sterile room with protesters outside won't work for her. It'll hurt her worse."

"For chrissakes, Keller," Monroe muttered.

The other uniformed guard muttered, "I hope you aren't seriously considering letting her go. She could be dangerous."

"Look, kid, you're new. I've worked with the Keller brothers for years and had no idea what they were capable of because they obviously expressed massive amounts self-control. If Dade says they can rehab her better at her home, I trust him."

"You trust him with the public's safety?"

"He's a damned good firefighter who has served his country on two tours. I trust him. And you—don't be like one of those protestors out there and ignore what you're seeing right in front of your face. You've been standing in the presence of two grizzly shifters, and neither one has eaten you yet. She's half-healed without assistance, and Dade wants to take care of his mate. Right? Did I say that right?"

"Yeah," Dade said, casting a worried glance at the window.

They argued on, but Quinn couldn't hear anything past the words "grizzly shifter" and "mate." She'd thought Dade was putting her on when he talked about changing into a bear, but no way were the cops in on the joke just for the benefit of a laugh at her. And those protesters outside were holding signs about caging people up. No, not people. Animals.

Dade was an animal.

Her breath stuttered in her throat as the Keller brothers entered the room again. "You weren't kidding?"

Dade flashed a frown as he grabbed a black

duffle bag off a chair in the corner. "About what?"

"About being a bear?"

"No, I wasn't kidding." His voice sounded exhausted as he pulled out a pair of cutoff jeans and an oversize navy T-shirt with the Breckenridge fire department logo in the upper corner.

"Boone, turn around."

His brother did, and Dade pulled the ties loose on the back of her hospital gown.

Quinn jerked away. "What are you doing?"

"Helping you undress."

Snatching the clothes from his hand, she said, "I can dress myself."

"Fine."

"Fine." She waited. "Turn around!"

Boone snorted a laugh from the other side of the room as Dade spun slowly to face the wall.

"Whose shirt is this?" It was large and fell around her knees. She tied it in a knot at her side so it wouldn't cover the short, cutoff denim and brush her injured legs.

"The shirt is mine, and the cutoffs I borrowed from my future sister-in-law, Rory. Moira will have to bandage you up again before we go."

The familiarity with which he spoke her name brought something foggy and green through her. "How do you know Moira?"

"She's—" Dade threw one of the cameras a quick glance and turned around just as she was trying to get the shorts over the burn marks on her legs.

Dade stepped forward until he was flush with her, then pulled outward on the hems of her shorts as she eased them over her legs so the fabric didn't touch her skin. Straightening, he whispered against her ear, "Moira is one of us."

His lips brushed her sensitive earlobe, and a shudder shook her spine and landed in her shoulders. Embarrassed by how easily he drew a reaction from her body, she dipped her gaze to hide the blazing heat in her cheeks.

When he eased back, a cocky smile ghosted his lips. "You ready?"

She nodded, afraid if she spoke her voice would crack on the emotion of how *not* ready she was to face the crowd outside.

"Maybe I should go alone. If all those people are here because of something to do with you, maybe it would be better if I just snuck out a back door."

The smile faded from his face. "They are at the back doors, too, and Quinn?"

"Yes?"

"They aren't here for me and Boone. They're here for you."

****

Dade stepped into the sunlight and shoved his sunglasses over his eyes to cover the feral color that would no doubt be there until he got Quinn somewhere safer. She'd been wary of his touch earlier, but now, he wrapped his hand around her smaller one and led her through the first line of news reporters.

"Are you angry with what he's done to you?" a woman called out, holding a microphone too close to Quinn's face.

"Did you shift in the hospital?" another yelled.

"Don't answer them," Dade growled out, shoving his way through the crowd.

"Have you ever killed anyone?" That one was directed at him, and he sure as shit wasn't admitting to his transgressions. All of his kills had been ordered by IESA or necessary when he'd served.

"Have you ever mauled a human while you were

a bear?" another asked.

Microphones were everywhere, and he ducked and weaved until the crowd surged in so close there was no pathway toward the black SUV that was waiting.

"Boone," he snarled.

"On it," his brother said.

Quinn made a pained noise behind him as she was pushed by a reporter who'd been shoved into her. "Hey!" he yelled as Boone skirted around him to clear a path. "Back the fuck off! She's hurt!"

"Dade," Quinn said on a breath. Her soft gray eyes were wide and frightened and something inside of him snapped.

"The next person to touch her is going to lose a fucking limb. Back. Off." He shoved a man who was being jostled into her and scooped Quinn up into his arms.

She buried her face against his chest as camera flashes surrounded them. Her arms went around his neck, and he held her closer as he made his way through the hole in the crowd Boone was unapologetically creating with his wide shoulders.

He settled her gently into the car, ignoring the

clawing hands at his back. Boone took the front seat with a somber expression, and when the doors were closed, the driver honked and began to make his way forward.

"Quinn," Dade said, drawing her attention from the masses outside the window. "This is Mason. His boss is a very powerful ally to shifters and has sent Mason to us as a bodyguard and driver when we need him."

"Damon Daye isn't just an ally," Boone muttered. "He's one of us."

"A shifter?" Quinn asked, the word sounding strange from her lips.

Dade sighed and nodded. "He's a much bigger shifter than we are."

Mason chuckled. "It's nice to meet you, Quinn."

She reached around the driver's seat and gripped his offered hand. "Nice to meet you, too. So, are you one of them too then? A bear shifter?"

Mason ran a meaty hand over his shaved head and took a sharp right onto the main road that bisected a stretch of piney wilderness. "Close, but no. I'm a boar shifter."

"A boar? Like a pig?"

"Ha!" Boone said from the front seat. "She just called you a pig shifter. Mason isn't one of those plump hams that roll around in the mud. Think more like the streamlined, wild predator with long tusks."

"Oh." The word came out as soft as a breath, and Dade squeezed her hand to reassure her she was safe.

"Moira said you don't remember much about what happened," Dade murmured.

The crowd thinned and Mason picked up speed.

"I remember the fire. And someone locking me in. Shayna, I mean. I never saw her. Has she been arrested?"

"She's in the wind, but don't worry about her," Mason said in a steely voice as he turned onto the main road lined with woods as far as the eye could see. "Mr. Daye has hired trackers to take care of her. She won't be bothering you anymore."

"Here," Boone said, handing Quinn his phone.

Dade fought the instinct to hide what he'd done for as long as possible. She'd find out eventually, though, and the sooner she dealt with what she'd become, the better.

She let his hand go to grip the phone in both palms. She hit the tiny triangle play button on the screen.

Footage from the local news station played, beginning with a somber woman reporting on "bear men" with supernatural abilities living among the general population. The video of Dade pulling her arm to his mouth and clamping down followed. A soft gasp left Quinn's lips as Dade began to strip off his turnout gear beside his brothers. The cell phone video wasn't the best quality, but it had picked up almost everything they'd said. When it panned to Quinn's Change, Dade turned away and looked out the window.

Cody had played the damned thing on repeat at the meeting he'd called, and there was only so many times he could watch Quinn suffer like that. The first Change was always the worst.

"Oh, God!" she cried. "That's not me. That's not me! I'm not that thing."

That *thing*. He was that thing. The disgust in her voice gutted him. He watched the passing lodgepole pine forest and agonized at the hitch in her voice. At the soft splat her tears caused against her legs. At the heartbreak in her voice when she asked, "Why? Why did you do put that thing inside of me?"

Swallowing his grief, he closed his eyes and shook his head. "I was trying to help."

"You've turned me into a freak, Dade! What kind of normal life can I lead now? Let me out. *Let me out*! Pull over, Mason." Panic laced every word, and her eyes darted wildly. She was cornered and scared, and a trapped, injured she-grizzly was the most dangerous kind.

"Do it," he murmured when Mason looked at him in the rearview with his dark eyebrows lifted high.

"Dade," Mason warned, "we've got two news vans behind us."

"Ooow," Quinn groaned, grabbing her middle. When she dragged her frightened gaze to him, her eyes were blazing green-gold, the mark of the Keller bears.

"You want to deal with a newly Changed grizzly in your nice ride, Mason?"

"Oh, here we go," Boone muttered. "I'll take care of the news crews. Just get her far into the woods or Cody is going to string us up."

"Well, he'll have to take a freaking number." The human lynch mob would be here shortly.

Dade pushed open the door as soon as Mason

slammed on the brakes. Quinn was shaking and pale as a phantom. The light freckles across her nose were stark against the porcelain color of her skin, and when she released her breath, it trembled.

"I don't feel well," she whispered, her eyes rimming with moisture.

Shit, this woman slayed him. He wanted to kill everything. Every. Single. Thing. And for what? She wasn't in danger from any outside source. She was in danger from the animal he'd put inside of her. Dade was grit—worse even.

Scooping her up, he swore, "Everything will be okay," but even he could hear the uncertainty in his voice.

He hadn't done this before, Changed someone. He hadn't ever wanted to. This wasn't something he wished on anyone, to spend the rest of their lives wrestling with a force of nature hidden away where people couldn't see the struggle.

Dade strode up the hill through the pine forest, Quinn in his arms as a screech of brakes sounded behind him. He cast a glance over his shoulder just in time to see Boone Change into his bear. Well, that was one way to distract the crowd. With a little luck, he wouldn't get shot this time.

A roar rattled the trees, and Quinn gasped and scrabbled out of his arms. "Is that Boone?" she asked, horror in her voice as she stared down the trail at his brother who was now scratching his back against a pine tree like he hadn't a care in the world. He was about to bore the shit out of the news crews. Dade would've laughed if Quinn's mouth wasn't hanging open in terror.

He bent to pick her up again, but she swatted his hand. "I can walk myself."

"But...your burns—"

"Don't hurt like they should. And yeah, I should probably be thanking you for whatever bear-man healing super powers you gave me because I saw my legs bent the wrong way under that beam and know what they felt like when that hot metal burned through me to the bone. And this," she said, waving her hands at the red, putty-like gashes across her legs, "is nothing compared to what I was supposed to deal with. I'm still angry, though, and I don't want you carrying me around like I'm helpless." She narrowed her eyes at him. "You think I'm weak, don't you?"

With a growl, Dade scrubbed his face and sidled

around her. He wasn't having their first spat within filming distance of the crews behind them.

"You do. You think because I had a soft heart at the vet clinic and that you caught me on a bad day and saw me cry a couple of times that I'm some sniveling, pathetic weak...human!"

"No, you're a bear shifter now."

"Eaaah!" she screeched. "I didn't ask for this, Dade."

He shook his head, fuming as they crested a hill. The news crews disappeared behind them, and now all he could hear was the soft noise of their vans and the cars coming up the road.

"You're walking too fast."

"I thought you didn't want me to coddle you." His angry words whipped past his lips, but when he turned, she was even paler than when they'd left the car. "Dammit, I'm sorry," he rushed out, gripping her under her elbows. He was emotional, and she threw him off-kilter every other minute, but the cold hard fact was she was still hurt and likely in shock from what she'd just learned.

"On the video, it seemed like you used me to come out to the public with what you are. Please tell me I'm not some springboard for your...people's...agenda. Please tell me my life will be normal again."

"My people are good, Quinn. They're families and hard workers who are just trying to make it, like everyone else. You weren't planned. I just couldn't watch you suffer knowing I could make it easier."

Her voice dipped to a ragged whisper as she leaned heavily on a tree. "This isn't easier."

"There wasn't time to get the human onlookers out of the way before I bit you." He held his hands out, pleading with her to try and understand. "I know I fucked up. Hell, I even knew it at the time, but I'd do it again. You were bad off. I didn't know if your back was broken, and I thought surely you had internal bleeding, and your breathing was so shallow. I've been around death, Quinn. Lots of it. You were toeing the line, and I didn't want to lose you before I even got to know you."

She inhaled deeply and shook her head. "So Moira was right. You did save me."

Dade shrugged. "Kind of."

"No, there's no kind of. You gave me the bear so I could live."

"I ruined your life with the bear so you could live."

Quinn looked defeated as she slunk down against the tree. She hissed as she brought her knees up to her chest.

Dade knelt in front of her and picked up a twig from the forest floor, snapped pine needles off it one by one. "I know I have no right to ask you now because you're still figuring out the hell I shoved you into, but someday, when I've worked hard enough for it, I'm going to beg your forgiveness."

"And someday," she whispered through a tremulous smile, "I'm going to give it to you."

"I won't let anything happen to you, Quinn. I swear it. My body was made to keep yours safe. You don't have to worry about any kind of danger, okay?"

She drew back, straightening her spine, as her delicate eyebrows arched. "No danger? Your neck, Dade. What happened to your neck?"

Dade bit back a curse as his mind revolted against the memories she scratched at. "One of the members of my Crew, Rory, was taken by a government agency that has been blackmailing me and my brothers into running missions for them.

Tours and black ops shit. Stuff I'm not allowed to talk about. They put trackers in our necks, and we wore them for years thinking they were just monitoring our vitals, hormones, location, that kind of stuff. What we didn't know is that the trackers were filled with acid and some agent that stopped the clotting of blood. It was a kill switch, and mine got pushed."

"Dade," she whispered. Her dove gray eyes were filled with horror when he dared to look at her.

"It doesn't even hurt anymore."

"Lie." Quinn looked down at her legs wrapped in bandages from her knees to her upper thighs. "Look. Now we match."

He shook his head to ward off the heartache in her words. "You should've never been involved in this. I knew you weren't strong enough for my world, and I followed you to your house, anyway. I should've let you keep your normal life."

"I knew it." She leaned her head back on the tree trunk, looking utterly drained. "I knew you thought I was weak. Well, I'm not. I'm soft-hearted, but I've been through worse than this."

He'd been in the middle of shifting his weight onto his other leg but froze. "What do you mean?"

Her smile was the saddest he'd ever seen. "I was married once."

"But not anymore?" The thought of her with anyone else felt like a hand clenching his heart.

"Jay served our country, like you. Only he didn't come back to me. I buried my new husband and mourned his life cut short beside his mother, and for years, I didn't let anyone touch my heart because the danger of losing anyone else was too big. And I survived all of that, so you see, I'm much stronger than you've given me credit for."

A surge of pride filled him as he shuffled closer and pulled her against his chest. She felt so good and warm in his arms. His heart was drumming against his sternum, and she could likely feel how affected he was against her cheek, but so what? She should see him. All of him. If she could share something so painful with him, she could have it all—if she wanted. His brave Quinn was strong, and he'd been a fool not to see it.

"I'm sorry," he whispered against her hair. "I'm sorry he didn't come back to you."

A soft sob left her lips, and she clutched onto his shirt and buried her face against his chest. "It's why I asked if you were still on active duty. I swore I'd learned my lesson, and now I'm choosing you. Army, black ops, secret missions, scars all over you that say you've paid for this life in blood, and I'm picking you despite it all. It's not your fault I'm here, Dade. I saw the video. Saw how raw your face looked as you were telling that paramedic I was yours. I know you were trying to help me. I'd planned on living a quiet life and clinging to my past with Jay, and you came and shook everything up. I'll be stronger."

"You are strong," he said thickly, heart in his throat. "I won't coddle you if you don't want. I have these stupid instincts to take care of you, and I will if you'll let me. But I swear I'll try to let you find your own way through this mess. You'll have to be patient with me, though. I haven't done this before."

"Done what?" she asked, sniffling and easing back. Her soft eyes were innocent as she asked him what this was between them.

"Felt this way about a woman. You've been married, and I can tell you loved Jay very much. You're my first, though, and I have all of these feelings and instincts keeping me off balance. I want to do every single thing for you and make you comfortable, but I can tell that is going to bother you. I'll figure it out, but it'll be easiest if you just tell me when I'm being a dumbass."

She snorted a laugh. "I'm not the best with cursing. Do you want me to use those actual words?"

"Yes," he said, relieved she could joke at a time like this. "Just say, Dade Leland Keller, you, sir, are being a dumbass."

"Leland?"

"It's a family name. All the Keller brothers' middle names are Leland."

"Oh," she mused. "Okay. Dade Leland Keller, you were a super dumbass the other day when you threw gravel on me while I was walking home with a flat tire."

"But not when I bit you?"

Quinn brushed her auburn waves behind her ears and studied him. "No. I understand why you did. I don't like it, but I get why you made that choice. Saving me isn't something I have to forgive you for. The rocks in my face though..."

A smile stretched Dade's face. "I'm sorry I did that. And I really liked the bacon you made me. Bears love bacon."

Quinn giggled a tinkling sound that filled his middle with warmth. It was the first time he'd heard her laugh, and it drew him back. He stroked a lock of her deep red hair that had fallen across her shoulder. "I like that."

"What?"

"I like that you can laugh even when the shit is hitting the fan."

"Well, I like that your muscles are big, and that you got all protective back there when those reporters got too rough."

"Mmm," he rumbled. "I like this game. Okay, I like the way your eyes have green in the middle of the gray, and I also like to think I'm the only one who's noticed that before."

"I like your scars. I think they make you look like a badass."

"I like your scars because they *make you* a badass."

Quinn was trying to hide a smile now, and her expression was so freaking cute he sat down and surrounded her with his long legs just to be closer to her.

"I like in the video when you took a bullet to

guard my body when I was turning into...you know."

"Say it."

She pursed her lips and lifted her chin. "A bear."

"I like that your bear has the same color fur as your hair."

"Oooh, you like redheads, do you?"

"And freckles."

"Oh, geez," she said, blushing from her neck to her hairline. "Okay, I feel better now, and we should probably get back to the car. We can continue this game when there isn't someone taking pictures from a few trees away." She waved to the paparazzi.

He'd heard him approach, but they weren't doing anything that would make Cody freak out if he saw it on the evening news tonight. Plus, he'd been having too much fun telling her the things he liked about her to care overly much. He had the distinct feeling this was going to be a part of life until the humans got used to the existence of shifters.

"Okay, I'm not supposed to coddle you, right?"

"Right."

Standing, he dusted the seat of his jeans until he'd loosed all the dried pine needles. "Fine, I won't even help you up."

"Dade!"

"Just kidding. Here."

She grinned, slid her palms against his, and warm tendrils reached up his arms where she touched him. He pulled gently, and then helped her back down the wooded hill toward the SUV.

Still pale and shaky, she followed slowly, but her determination to be strong and do it on her own only made him like her more.

Ten minutes alone with her, and he'd already learned so much. No more imagining what she was like. She was a bear shifter now, and even though she had no clue what it meant, she was his claim. Quinn didn't know it yet, and he was determined to take this slow and give her time, but she was it for him.

No matter what came their way now, he was going to make sure she was safe, and that Quinn knew she was cared for.

EIGHT

Quinn couldn't quit sneaking little glances at Dade as he drove them away from her house. Was she scared of what was happening? Heck yeah. But everything seemed less overwhelming when he was around.

The man spoke with such confidence and seemed to know exactly how to handle every situation that came their way. He could've told her to buck up in the car earlier and pipe down until they got somewhere far away from the news crews, but she had been on the verge of something big. Her insides had been burning, and her blood had hummed just under her skin with the need to do…something. And Dade had known just how to put her at ease.

He wasn't the rude, confounding man she'd thought he was. Sure, he was a dangerous sort of creature. Nothing screamed that more than his scars, the inhuman, lithe grace in his gait, and the steely, humorless looks he could give in an instant. And she was pretty sure he would've made good on his oath and ripped someone's limb off outside of the hospital earlier, but with her, he was gentle and accommodating.

He was a powerhouse, practically reeking of dominance, but he was aiming that bubble of protection he could provide right at her. It made it really hard to resent the feral side of her protector. She wanted to know everything about him. His dodging questions about his scars and missions only made her want to be closer to him. She had a natural curiosity and desire to dig deeper into what made Dade tick. And whatever that said about her, she didn't care.

There was something basic between them. Some chemical connection on a cellular level that made her want to touch him and be near him. Maybe it was science or some instinctive compatibility of their basic natures. Perhaps it was that he was part animal, and she understood him better than most people she'd met—she didn't know. All she knew was when she was around him, he made her want to be braver and better. He made her stomach do curious flip-flops, and for the first time in a long time, the thought of a future with a man made her pulse race with excitement over the unknown.

"Are you sure you're okay with me crashing at your place?" she asked in a much smaller voice than she'd intended. Waves of random shyness did that to her. Apparently, the grizzly sleeping inside of her didn't do much for bolstering her confidence around intimidating, sexpot shifters like Dade Leland Keller.

"Of course I'm sure. I don't think I could handle you staying in town without the protection of the Breck Crew right now. I'd be there watching over your house from the uncomfortable seat in my truck and putting us both at risk by allowing us to be separated from our people."

Our people. That was insane to think about. She had people, and she didn't even know them yet. A sense of excitement and terror unfurled in her stomach, and she clenched her hands against the urge to panic, or squeal or both. "When will I meet the rest of the Breck Crew?"

"Tomorrow if you want. Ma has already sent me about thirty text messages asking about you. I think she'd given up on me ever finding a mate."

"Mate," she whispered, testing out the word on her tongue. Simultaneously, it sent a trill of intimidation and elation through her, leaving her breathless.

"Sorry. I know humans don't talk like that. Sometimes I forget that you're new to this because you seem to be handling it so well. We don't have to talk about that stuff until you're ready."

She drew up straight at the realization she was kind of handling this like a champion. The animal lover in her was just as accepting of her new inner furry rider as it was scared for her future. She'd been on a roller coaster of emotions with all of this, but a small, quiet part of her felt right at home with her new animal side. "What does being your mate mean?"

Dade huffed a laugh and rubbed his hands over his platinum blond hair, spiking it up everywhere. It seemed to be a nervous habit of his, one that made this big tough guy even more endearing to her. "I don't really know. I was planning on calling my half-brother about it tonight after you fell asleep."

"What do you feel?"

Dade screwed up his face and shook his head. "If I tell you, you'll run for the hills and never look back."

Quinn held back a squeak in her throat at how cute he was. "Well, now you have to tell me."

"Swear that anything I say in this car doesn't make it back to my brothers or their mates. Or Ma."

"Fine." Easy promise. She didn't even know his family other than Boone. She pulled her duffle bag of clothes tighter against her side and settled against the passenger seat cushion of his truck. Outside, it was late in the evening and the fireflies were just coming out, illuminating the piney woods with little blinks of light. It was beautiful, but not as alluring as watching Dade's profile as he struggled to find words. Chiseled jaw adorned with the beginnings of that short, blond beard, as if he hadn't bothered to shave since she'd been taken to the hospital. The thick chords of muscle in his throat moved when he swallowed, and when he ghosted her an are-you-sure-you're-ready-for-this look, his aqua-colored eyes were worried. That he was concerned with what she thought of him was baffling.

Him, a big, dominant bear shifter who'd survived God knows what, and he was worried about what she, a quiet, mildly clumsy widow, thought of him.

"When I first saw you, my bear woke right up. It was this there-she-is moment, and you were sitting on the floor of the vet's room, mourning something I didn't understand, and all I wanted to do was make it better. But right before I'd gone in there, Shayna had stopped me on the side of the road, threatened a girl I used to hang out with, and I'd just got done swearing up and down that I'd never put a living soul in that woman's path. And then there you were, not fifteen minutes later. And then when I heard the vet tell you to take the rest of the day off, I got this jumpy feeling inside. I stalled paying for Tank's check-up so you'd have time to gather your stuff and head out, because even though I had just told myself I wouldn't get involved with anyone, I was already planning to see you again. And you were so upset, and your tire was flat, and I wanted to put your bike in the back of my truck and ask you out. Take you to a movie or dinner or something. But Shayna was there tailing me, reminding me I couldn't have anything that I wanted without it being ripped away from me, just like the agency she works for has always done to me and my crew."

"Is that why you ignored me for that whole week?"

"Exactly why. And it wasn't easy, woman. You'd already made your mark on me. I threw myself into work up at the firehouse, but I couldn't keep you off my mind for long. I wanted to know you. Know what you were doing and if you were seeing anyone. I wanted to know what you liked to do outside of work."

She grinned and looked pointedly in the back seat where Daffodil and Beans were snuggled up together in the crate they shared. "Did you imagine you'd be shacking up with me and two frilly dogs by the end of the next week?"

"Now, *that* I didn't imagine. I pegged you for a cat person for some reason."

"Daffodil can't handle cats. I fostered one once, and my dog got bullied relentlessly."

"Well, she's three pounds of submissive. She didn't stand a chance with a cat. What the hell is going on here?" he asked, leaning forward.

Red and blue flashed across his face, and Quinn stretched her neck to look out the front window. A crowd was gathered at the mouth of a fork in the road. Some held signs, and some seemed to be trying to hold others back. A police barricade covered the entrance to a poorly fenced property.

"The police around here have better things to do than babysit our land," Dade muttered as he pulled through.

He rolled down the window. "Hey, Monroe." Something hit the back of the truck and Dade threw the crowd behind him a pissed off glare. "I thought they kept our names out of the press."

The dark-haired officer from the hospital nodded and gave him an empty smile. "This isn't the national news's doing, I'm afraid. A couple of bloggers in Breckenridge interviewed the witnesses from the fire. Your names leaked online." He jerked his chin at the restless crowd. "They've been at this for hours. Sorry, Dade. If you don't want to stay closer to the station, we'll have to camp out here until these yahoos get bored. Cody is posting no trespassing signs to protect your property, but I wouldn't advise going after anyone who slips through, and especially not as an animal. Everyone is waiting for you to screw up. Don't give them the satisfaction, yeah?" Monroe patted the open window and nodded a greeting to Quinn. "Y'all have a good night. We'll be out here if you need us."

"Mmm," Dade murmured. "You know I'm sorry for this, man. I wish what we were didn't stir everyone up."

"It'll be a tornado at first, but the storm will pass eventually."

Dade gave a two fingered wave to a tall, muscular man who was nailing a *No Trespassing* sign onto the rundown fence beside the road. Quinn recognized him from the video.

"Is that Cody?" she asked.

"The one and only."

As they began to pull away, she asked, "And he's your alpha, right?"

"Nah." Dade kept his troubled eyes straight ahead on the road. "Cody is *our* alpha."

"Oh. So we're his servants?"

"No, woman, you won't bow down to anyone unless Cody is making an important decision for our crew. He's a good leader with a good head on his shoulders."

"Maybe we should stop so I can introduce myself."

"That'll slow him down, and he has a family to get home to. You'll meet him tomorrow."

"Okay." She waved to him, anyway.

Cody nodded once and raised a hammer in the air, then turned back to his work.

Quinn fidgeted with the strap of her duffel bag. "He's out here because of me," she murmured, settling back into her seat.

"No, he's not. We discussed going public before you were even on my radar. I get your need to take credit for bad things happening. I have the same instinct, but this one isn't on you."

"Why would you want to go public? Your kind has stayed hidden all this time. Why now?"

"*Our* kind. And the answer to that is IESA."

"What's that?"

"The International Exchange of Shifter Affairs. They are a secret arm of the government that has been flexing its muscles with us for a while. With lots of shifter crews actually, and it's not just bears. Their leader, Krueger, pressed on the Breck Crew for two generations. He hit the kill switch on my dad while he was working a fire, made it look like an accident. We didn't figure that out until he hit my kill switch, though. Our chemical burns looked the same and were both on our necks. When shifters lost their usefulness, they came up missing, or if they cut their trackers out of their throats, IESA sent us in."

"What do you mean? Like, you were a clean-up crew?"

"Unintentionally. After me and my brothers served, we came back with a special set of skills. Combine that with our healing and shifter strength, and Krueger recruited us for missions we were made to believe were for protecting the public. A couple of weeks back, though, Cody and I went on a mission with a target that didn't feel right, and we found out we'd been hunting shifters the whole time. Putting innocent marks down, thinking we were still serving our country. And yeah, we didn't have much choice in it. Krueger threatened the crew's cubs, Gage's mate, Ma, Rory. It doesn't change that we were the ones who pulled the trigger time and time again. I don't think the government meant for Krueger to take the liberties he did with us. I think he did things on the sly, and they lost control of him. At least, that's what I hope. Cody wanted to come out because we went to war with IESA a couple of weeks back, and now the woman who hurt you, Shayna, is rebuilding it from the ground up." He cast her a quick glance. "As you can imagine, we aren't thrilled about going back to the way it was. Krueger wasn't going to stop until we were all dead, and now Shayna is just as vindictive."

"Holy moly," Quinn said on a breath, facing forward again. "How many people did you have to kill?"

Dade shook his head tightly. "I can't, Quinn. I'm haunted enough without recalling my ghosts."

"I'm sorry," she whispered. "I won't ask about that anymore, but if you want to talk about it, I won't run."

"You would. If you knew the real me, you wouldn't be able to stomach being in the same room."

His words filled her with a numbing sadness. How could he say that? He'd sacrificed so much at the hands of horrid people, and he was still standing. Sure, he'd done awful things to survive, but he hadn't chosen to. He hadn't known his marks weren't a threat. He'd been lied to and manipulated, and now those lost lives were gashes on his soul, lined up so he could feel the eternal pain of each target he'd taken. She hated Krueger. Hated IESA. Hated Shayna. "It's not fair."

"Life isn't fair."

She bit her thumbnail and looked out the window. "Despise yourself all you want to, Dade. I saw you cradling your dog last week while he got his shots. I saw the pity in your eyes when I was crying on the floor. I heard Monroe talk about all the people you've saved fighting fires. I'm alive right now because you were cool with putting your entire crew at risk to save me. Everyone has dark places in them, myself included. It matters what you do to keep those shadows small. Try to convince yourself all you want to that you're too damaged for me to accept." She swung her gaze to him. "I'm still proud that you're mine."

He took his eyes off the fork in the dirt road once, then twice, his eyes steady on her, as if he was waiting for her to take it back. "You aren't thinking right. It's been a long day and a lot has happened—"

"Why are you trying to convince me of what I can and can't accept, Dade? Is this your way of trying to chase me off of anything real with you?"

"No," he said, shaking his head for emphasis. "That's not what I want. I just want you to go into this with your eyes wide open." He pulled to a stop in front of a dark cabin and turned to face her. "This is a shock to me, as well. You asked what being mated feels like to me, and it scares the shit out of me, Quinn. Truly. I've lived all this time responsible for myself and for my crew, and that's it. Chasing a bond wasn't something that ever crossed my mind."

"You've been with other women. A man like you…" She frowned. "I know you've had relationships with other women."

"No, I've had sex with women. Empty sex. I haven't ever stayed until breakfast, and now I feel like I want to pledge my entire life to you. It has my head all messed up."

"I've only been with Jay."

Dade went rigid, equal parts horror and confusion in his eyes. "What do you mean?"

"I mean, I've only slept with Jay, and the first time wasn't until our wedding night. Not for any reason other than we wanted to wait and make it special."

"More proof," Dade said in a hoarse voice, "that I'm a terrible match for you."

"You should've worked through that before you made me care for you!" Quinn flung the words at him, then slid from his pickup and climbed the porch stairs. Chin lifted high, she waited at the front door for him to let her in.

Dade sat in the truck, gripping the wheel, eyes downcast. Good. He should feel like worm slime after trying to push her away like that. She could practically see the war he waged within himself to keep her close or to keep her at arm's length, but he needed to pick a side. She'd known love. The good kind where she and Jay had respected each other and talked through their problems.

Dade was a different beast altogether.

She could be patient and wait for him to come around, but ultimately, he would have to be the one to decide whether to jump all in or not.

Dade shut the truck door a little too firmly. Gravel shuffled behind her, and his shoes made hollow sounds on the stairs as he strode toward where she stood on his darkened porch. She closed her eyes as a delicious wave of warmth crashed through her middle when he reached around her to unlock the door. He smelled amazing, like soap and pine sap, and something heady that belonged only to Dade.

He pushed open the door and took the duffle bag from her, then flipped a light switch inside. She gasped in surprise as she did a slow circle in the living room to take it all in. The cabin was small—one of those big front porch, tin roof, log siding models. But inside, the space was so open it looked much larger than from the outside. Wood walls, wood floors, an old fashioned stone hearth, sparse furnishings, and dark light fixtures gave the home a mannish feel. In the kitchen, the appliances were stainless steel, a contrast to the old-timey wooden cabinets and countertops. Along the back wall over the kitchen was a set of stairs that led to a single door.

She rented a cabin just outside of town, but it didn't have character like this home did.

Dade busied himself with folding a blue and orange blanket that had been left wadded on the dark leather couch, but every few seconds, he cast his eyes her way, as if he needed to see her reaction to his place.

"This place is amazing. And unexpected."

"How so?" Dade asked, draping the folded blanket across the back of the couch.

"Well, you're a bachelor. I thought there would be dishes stacked high in the sink and TV trays of old microwave dinners sitting out."

Dade smiled and hooked his hands on his hips. "Ma didn't raise a slob. If she came over and my place was a mess, I'd have to hear about it for a week. Besides, I like my living space tidy. My bear gets restless around clutter. I start feeling like I need to come up with escape plans." He dropped his gaze. "That sounds weird."

"No, it doesn't. You've been through a difficult life and have had to hide what you are. My new instincts are overwhelming. I can't imagine what it's been like for you, but your animal liking a tidy home isn't weird."

Dade's blond brows drew down as if he was uncomfortable with the turn in conversation, so she gave him an out. "Where is your bathroom? It's been a long day, and I want to clean up."

"I don't like this," he murmured. Dragging sad

eyes to her, he said, "I screwed up in the truck. I let the conversation turn, and before that, we'd been having fun. I got in my own head, and now you're talking to me like we're strangers again. And I don't like that." His voice dipped lower. "I like when you are smiling and happy with me."

"Well, I like when you aren't trying to push me away."

His chest heaved as he inhaled a deep breath. Nodding his head toward the stairs, he said, "I'm going to make you some dinner. Food, meat especially, will help you heal faster. Take your time."

Quinn padded up the stairs and made her way through the door. His room was like the rest of the house, tidy and clean, not even a streak of dust on his dresser. His bed, however, was covered in jumbled sheets and a dark, disheveled comforter, as if he'd slept rough last night.

With a grin, she spun and landed on the soft mattress. Rolling on her side, she inhaled his pillow. Some of her new bear powers were pretty cool. Imagining the monster that would rip out of her again in a week or so was terrifying, but being able to smell every detail on Dade, to be able to pick his scent out of all the rest, was awesome.

"Are you sniffing my bed?" Dade's deep voice sounded from the doorframe.

With a squeak, Quinn sat up and clutched her chest. She shot a horrified glance at the bed, imagining how ridiculous she must have looked, then scrunched up her nose. "I'm sorry."

Dade pushed off the frame where he'd been leaning and approached slowly, as if he was stalking prey. "You don't have to say sorry for anything, woman. I came up here to apologize and found you on my bed, looking hot as hell in those little cutoff shorts."

The heat in her neck drove up to the tips of her ears. She probably looked like a ruddy tomato right now. "The bandages take away from my sex appeal."

"Says who?" he asked, pulling her ankles until her backside hit the edge of the bed. He placed her palm against the rigid roll of his erection pressed against the seam of his jeans. "I think your sex appeal is just fine."

Dade knelt in between her legs.

"What are you doing?" she asked, jerking her knees in reflexively and bumping his ribs.

Dade pressed her thighs wider and said, "Not what you obviously think I'm doing. I'm going to take your bandages off because I want to show you something."

"Okay," she said softly.

Dade canted his head, eyes serious. "You ever had a man eat you before, Quinn?"

Her breath caught at his dirty words. Heat pooled between her legs just thinking about his head bobbing between her thighs. "No." She and Jay had been young, and he'd never offered.

"Mmm," he said, tugging at the bandage on her right leg and unrolling it slowly. "If you ever want me to, just say the word. I've been wanting to taste you since I met you."

"That sounds uncomfortable for you. I'd...feel bad asking."

Dade laughed and folded up the first bandage, then removed a long pad of gauze Moira had put over the burn. "It would be my fuckin' pleasure to make you come with my tongue. I bet you'd be a noisy little thing." His hungry eyes held her frozen in his gaze, churning blue-green that dipped her stomach to her toes. "Now, look at what your bear has done for you."

She gasped at the pink scar across her thigh. It barely hurt past a dull ache anymore and looked weeks old. "I don't understand. I knew I was healing fast, but this is insane." She scrabbled to remove the other bandage, and when it was in a little pile on the bed beside her, she looked in amazement at the matching scar on her other leg.

Dade ran his fingertip along the line of the mark on her right leg, conjuring gooseflesh with his touch. "Damn, woman. You're gorgeous."

"Even scarred?"

"Especially scarred. Tell me, why were you so far away from the door when I found you?"

She shook her head as emotion crashed over her at the memory of that awful fire. "The cats," she whispered. "They were so scared. I could hear someone banging on the door, trying to let me out, but the cats were screaming, and I thought if the wall caved, they could maybe get out. I was opening their cages when the beam fell from the ceiling."

Dade gripped her knees and spread her legs wide, then brushed his lips against the sensitive skin of her inner thigh. "I knew it as soon as the cats ran past my legs. I knew you'd taken a risk to save them.

Brave, selfless, beautiful woman."

Quinn exhaled slowly, her breath shaking as she leaned back on locked arms and let him kiss her other leg. His soft smacking sounds pooled wetness between her legs. "If we do this, you're in this with me. No half-in, trying to convince us both we're not right together."

Dade's eyes snapped up to hers, and a slight frown took his face. "Quinn, we don't have to go that far right now. You and Jay took your time, and I can wait, too."

Heat flooded her cheeks. "I thought you said I was your mate."

"You are."

"That sounds serious."

"It is."

"Then I'm asking you."

Dade's eyebrows arched high, and two dimples bracketed his sensual lips as he offered her a surprised smile. "Asking me what?"

"I'm asking you to be with me. Not just intimately either. I want to feel like you have my back, no matter what we go through with shifters coming out to the public. I want to know in my heart you will be there for me, like I'll be there for you."

"Quinn, sex doesn't have anything to do with that."

She smiled sadly and pulled at his shirt until it came off his head, leaving his hair mussed. His skin was smooth between the shrapnel scars. She understood now how big an injury had to be to leave a mark like that on a bear shifter, and he'd somehow survived everything that had marred his body. She traced the chemical burn on his throat, and this time he allowed it, though his eyes lost their smile. "You've trained yourself to not feel sex, Dade. It has to be different with me. I want all of you. I don't want you to fuck me like you've trained yourself to do with other women. I want you to *feel* me."

At her words, he weaved like a drunk man, his eyelids closed half-mast, and now his hands were stroking up and down her legs rhythmically as if he didn't know he was even doing it.

"I want you to stay for breakfast," she whispered.

"I won't be any good at this."

She leaned down and kissed the burn on his throat, then whispered in his ear, "Make me come slow."

"Fuuuck," he said on a sigh, pupils dilated. Stretching up, he kissed her.

His lips turned soft in an instant and molded to the shape of hers. His thumb drew little circles just under the hem of her knotted up shirt, and when he pressed the palm of his hand upward and against the flat plane of her back, she gasped and arched toward him. His touch brought fire in its wake, igniting her nerve endings. She'd always been sensitive to touch, but with Dade, it was different. It was more.

He pulled her hips closer until she hovered at the edge of the mattress, until his taut torso pressed against her sex. Rolling her hips gently, she bit her lip as her clit brushed against her jeans.

She'd pulled her hair back in a ponytail earlier, but now Dade reached behind her and tugged the hair band from her locks, freeing them. He lifted the hem of her shirt, then tugged it over her head and unsnapped her bra with a practiced *snick* of his fingers.

She closed her eyes for a moment, hoping he would like what he saw. For years, she hadn't been bare in front of a man, asking them to enjoy her body. And even then, it had been Jay, who she'd known for years. When she opened her eyes, Dade was drinking her in with a stunned gaze that settled her thumping heart. The corner of his lip turned up slightly, then fell as he lifted his eyes to hers. "You're perfect."

She traced a moon-shaped scar on his shoulder and whispered, "So are you."

He cupped her head and kissed her again, slowly this time, gently sucking her bottom lip before easing back and then kissing her again. She loved him as he was, wild and on edge, but Dade like this, tender and affectionate, plucked at her heartstrings and attached them to him, one by one.

He trailed soft kisses down her throat as his hand gently pressed her lower back until she bowed closer to him. His taut chest was warm against her. Lips soft, he pulled her nipple into his mouth and lapped at her gently. She ran her fingertips through his hair and watched his jaw move as he brushed his tongue against her sensitive skin, his sensual affection pooling wetness between her legs. When he looked back up at her, the fire had died from his eyes, and only adoration remained. Slowly, he unsnapped his jeans, then pushed them down until they joined their shirts on the floor. Taking his time, he pulled at her shorts, careful they didn't touch the scars that should've been painful if Dade hadn't saved her from the burning. Her panties tickled her ankles just before he pulled them off. Tiny kisses brushed the inside arch of her foot as he worshipped her. Soft bites trailed up the inside of her leg, and when he reached her scars again, he touched his lips to the fevered flesh on both legs, soothing the burn with his attention.

Outside, the crickets and cicadas sang a quiet soundtrack for this moment that was shattering all the walls she'd erected around her heart. Dade ran his fingertips up the sides of her legs. His short whiskers tickled her stomach as he pressed his lips on the soft area right above her hips. He seemed as thirsty for her skin as she was for his, exploring her with his mouth and touch. She understood. She couldn't stop rubbing the skin of his back and running her fingers through his short hair. Petting, adoring, discovering her mate in that slow way that drew her heart into her throat and made her feel like she was falling all at once.

Eyes on hers, Dade stood slowly and settled her back against the mattress. The nervous flutters in her stomach washed away as he covered her with his body, skin warm down the length of her. She rubbed her leg against his, and a soft rumbling noise rattled from his chest.

"Sorry," he whispered, as if any volume to his voice would break the magic of this moment.

"Don't apologize," she said, matching his quiet tone. "She pressed her hand against his chest, just over his heart as the sound rattled him again, softer this time. "I like that you can be yourself with me. We're the same now, you and me. No more hiding."

Dade searched her face and nodded. "No more hiding," he repeated.

The swollen head of his cock brushed her wet seam, and she spread her legs instinctively, ready for him. "Please," she begged as he eased back. "I want to feel you."

With a helpless noise in his throat, Dade cupped the back of her neck and pushed a strand of loose hair away from her face. With a slow, powerful thrust of his hips, he slid into her, gaze never letting her go.

He filled her, stretched her, made her feel whole and steady in ways she hadn't experienced before. "I'm falling," she whispered.

His lips turned up in a ghost of a smile just before he kissed her. His tongue brushed hers as he pushed into her again. "Me, too."

Teeth grazing her lips, soft sexy noises in his throat, hips rolling slowly, eyes on her, always on her. Dade was hers now. Arching her back, she relaxed her muscles as he pushed into her so deeply he brushed the oversensitive place between her legs. Gentle grip on her hair, his thumb stroked her bottom lip as he leaned in to kiss her again, his graceful body warming hers, covering hers, protecting hers. She was safe here with him. Safe in his arms. Coveted against these sheets in the eyes of the man she was falling into, falling for, falling with. Pushing in, easing out, building the inferno inside of her. Pressure stretched from her middle until she gasped out his name. So close.

His arms trembled and his breath shook as he drank her in, watching her, touching her reverently. Gripping his wrists, desperate to keep his touch close, she bucked against him and closed her eyes as soft crashing waves pulsed around his swollen shaft. She opened her eyes to watch him, this beautiful, masculine, feral man who was showing her how tender he could be.

His hips rocked faster against hers. Three more strokes, and he brushed his teeth against her shoulder, then searched her eyes. God, she wished he could see himself through her eyes. Strong, loyal...loved. Dade froze, muscular arms flexed as he groaned. Warmth filled her in hot jets as he bucked into her, and as he throbbed inside of her, matching her own release, he cupped her face like she was precious, and kissed her lips softly with his own.

Quinn ran her nails up and down his back as they lay there, tangled up together, bodies melded, kisses gentle. The first tear slipped the corner of her eye before she even realized she was crying.

Easing back, Dade wicked the drop of moisture away and frowned. Still whispering in the soft light of his room, he asked, "Are you okay?"

She nodded and let off a thick laugh. She pulled his palm to her mouth and let her lips linger there as she tried to get ahold of her emotions. "I'm just happy is all."

Smiling, Dade pulled out of her slowly, then rolled off beside her. Pulling her back against his chest, he wrapped his arms around her middle and kissed the back of her neck. "I'm happy, too."

His satisfied sigh tickled her shoulder blades, and when she stretched back against him like an overgrown cat, he pressed his lips against her hair. His warmth disappeared from her back for a moment, and a country song sounded from his stereo before he returned and pulled her more firmly against his chest.

Soft guitar notes filled the air as a crooner sang about a woman with a wild spirit he'd fallen in love with.

"Mmm, I like this song," she said languidly.

"What else do you like?"

She frowned at the wall, trying to come up with a good answer. "You know, it has been so long since anyone asked me about myself. And now it feels like there is nothing interesting about me."

"That's not true at all," Dade murmured, plucking her earlobe gently with his lips. "I want to know everything. I want to know what made you into this shy, caring woman."

"I like animals."

"That's a given."

"And I like riding my bike. I like being outdoors.

And I like…I like you." Her voice faded to a whisper.

"You said you mourned Jay with his mother. What about your mother? Was she there for you?"

Quinn gritted her teeth and closed her eyes at the momentary slash of pain through her insides. "I don't have a mother, or a father. And it's not some tragic tale of losing them or anything like that before you start thinking I'm pitiful. They gave me up for adoption when I was five."

"Jesus. Do you remember them?"

"I know I'm supposed to, because I was old enough, but I really don't. I mean, no blurry faces in my dreams or anything. I just sort of…let them go."

"Who raised you?"

"I was in the foster care system until I was released at eighteen. The last ten years were spent with one family though, and it wasn't so bad. A woman named Meryl Brady took me in, along with a revolving plethora of other foster kids. And she wasn't one of those people trying to scam the government for money, either. She got paychecks for us, but she put that money straight back into feeding us and buying us clothes and getting us school supplies. It was a situation where the older kids raised the younger ones because her husband had passed away, and she was working two jobs to make ends meet. Sometimes I think that's maybe why I tend to be quieter. There were a lot of loud personalities in that house, and the cast never stayed the same for long. I was a little overwhelmed with everything, I think. Anyway, it wasn't a bad childhood. Not like it could've been. It was different from most people's, but it was all I knew, so I didn't feel jipped or anything."

"When did you meet Jay?"

An accidental smile took her face. "Freshmen year of high school. He was the complete opposite of me. Loud, never met a stranger, talked to everyone, and seemed to remember every detail about his conversations with them. He was athletic and played sports, and I was a quiet geek who was so clumsy I could barely walk in a straight line. I don't know why he took an interest in me. I think over the four years we dated and the year we were married, I didn't ever come to grips with why a boy like him would look twice at a girl like me. I'm still a little baffled when I think about the girls that flocked him. He could've slept with anyone in that school, but he chose to wait for me."

She sighed as pain unfurled in her chest. "I moved in with his mother, Ruth, when he joined the army. If I ever had a mother, I think Ruth was the closest. We both answered the door when they told us Jay had been killed in combat, and I held her hand all during the funeral. We were both a mess, but we kept each other strong enough to get through it while everyone was giving their condolences. And we fell apart together when we'd been left to our grief. She didn't have a husband, and all the sudden, she didn't have a son anymore, either. And I'd lost my whole world, too. I still talk to her. She was the one who told me to move out here and start fresh. She was worried I'd never move on. I moved out right after the funeral and got a job waiting tables, but she said I deserved a better life and offered to pay for my vet tech school. Right before I moved here, she made a big home cooked meal and had me over. It was hard going over to her house after Jay passed. She kept his room just the same, and her walls were covered in his pictures. She had turned her home into a memorial, while I hid everything that reminded me of him so it wouldn't hurt so bad. But I went for dinner, and I didn't even cry when she told me she was afraid I'd never move on from Jay and I would end up just like her—alone. She said it was her biggest fear, and she wanted me to learn to live again because Jay wouldn't have liked me moping about for him after so much time. It's just..." She swallowed a lump that had formed in her throat. "It's just hard to move on sometimes, you know?"

Several quiet heartbeats of time passed as he stroked his fingertips up and down the curve of her waist. "I don't think I've ever felt anything that deeply. Not loss or joy or love or anything. Not until I met you. I think maybe you are a much better person than I am, Quinn."

"You love your family."

"I do, but I don't remember crying at my dad's funeral. I didn't cry when we found out he'd had an affair either, even though my brothers were pissed. I didn't feel betrayed or anything. Just saw it as getting a surprise half-brother. I looked up to Bruiser just as much as I looked up to my other brothers. Still do."

"You're the baby of the family?"

Dade ran his fingers through her hair, smoothing the tresses before pressing his lips against her neck.

"I am. Ma used to try and coddle me relentlessly, and I remember I would get so mad. I wanted to be tough and immovable like my brothers, so I trained myself not to be affected. I became the get-shit-done member of our family. And when things went bad, I forced myself not to feel anything. I just looked for solutions and tried to find ways to get my family out of whatever shit storm we were weathering. And after a while, it was easy. Life was easier because I had no feelings when I took out our targets. Other soldiers struggled, hell, even my brothers struggled when we went overseas to fight, but I didn't. It was just a place to be at the time, and the danger part was something I was already used to. I was a bear shifter in Krueger's sites. My shelf life wasn't going to be a long one, so I lived like I was already dead."

"What about when you got your scars. Were you scared then?"

"No. Just hurt and ready to not feel the pain anymore. *Feeling* was an irritant, like an itch deep in my muscle or a splinter in my hand I couldn't reach."

"You feel now, though. I see how much your eyes have softened up. When did that happen?"

He was quiet so long she thought he wouldn't

answer, so she rolled over and snuggled her cheek against his chest.

"You'll think it's silly," he murmured.

"I swear I won't."

Dade rested his chin on top of her head and inhaled deeply before releasing a long breath. "Cody chose Boone over me, and I was hurt for the first time in a really long time."

"How did he choose Boone?"

We were in this barn Krueger had lured us to by kidnapping Cody's mate, Rory. We all had the trackers in our necks, but Cody had the only knife to cut them out. I know Boone was right beside Cody, so it made sense that he cut his out first, but there was still this part of me that wondered if he'd chosen my brother to save first for a deeper reason. Like, maybe Boone was more valuable or Cody cared about him more."

"Dade, I don't think that's it. I think he just made a split second decision in the heat of battle."

"I know. That's why I haven't pissed and moaned about it to him, but I was bleeding out, and it hurt so bad and that's just where my mind went. I told you it was stupid. If you saw Cody's hand, you'd think I was an ass for even bringing it up. My kill switch was detonated while he was pulling it from my neck. The acid burned us both. I'm alive because he didn't care about his own skin as much as saving me."

"You know it's okay to feel emotional about that time though, right? Maybe you should talk to Cody about how you felt. Maybe it'll be better if you get it out into the open with your brother."

"Nah. I feel better saying it to you, but I can't imagine it would make anything easier by putting more guilt onto my brother's shoulders. As the alpha, he carries a bigger burden than the rest of us. We all lived. That's what matters."

"You are a strong man, Dade Leland Keller."

"Mmm, I used to be. Now, I don't know what I am anymore. You've got me all mixed up."

"No," Quinn said, pressing her lips against his collar bone, "I'm making you feel again. That's not a bad thing." She smiled as she traced a long, curved scar on his chest. "Welcome back to the land of the living."

NINE

Quinn didn't know it, but she owned him completely.

Dade watched her sleep in the dark before dawn, propped up on his elbow so he could see the soft curve of her face better. Long, graceful neck, auburn waves fanned out across the pillow, fair skin, light freckles across her nose and shoulders. From here he could make out the curve of her waist and hips under the sheets. God, he loved her. If she knew how devoted to her he already was, she'd run scared.

But maybe not.

She'd woken up an hour ago when he'd adjusted his arm over her back. She'd rolled to face him, snuggled into his arms, and whispered that she loved him.

The last cold shards of his heart had melted with her admission. No longer was he a man who only lived to survive and protect the Breck Crew. Quinn now fell under his protection. His body was hers, made to protect her.

Deep gray streaked across the sky out the window, but the stars were still out, winking at him as if they'd known all along Quinn was going to come in and shake him to his core.

Daffodil woofed softly from beside the bed, and Dade froze a split second before he heard it. A soft, long *creak* sounded from the stairway outside the door.

Someone was in the house.

In one smooth motion, Dade reached over Quinn's sleeping form and pulled a long, curved knife from under the mattress. Muscles tensed and ready, he padded silently to the door and pressed his back against the wall beside it.

The door opened without a sound, and Dade's heart pounded like a war drum as his eyes followed a handgun that lifted slowly, aimed at his mate as she slept.

Fury blasted through his veins, washing everything in a red tint. With a feral snarl in his throat, Dade jerked the attacker's wrist upward. The blast of gunfire was deafening. Sheetrock exploded from the ceiling where the bullet landed, showering him in chalky dust as he whipped around the door and drew his blade down the thin wrist of their assailant, careful to nick the tendon.

Shayna screamed as she dropped the weapon from her ruined grip. The gun clattered to the wooden floorboards as Dade ducked her elbow and rammed her against the wall. Her knee came straight up into his ribcage, but he was too far gone in his fury to feel pain now.

This was the woman who'd helped IESA put tracker kill switches inside of him and his family. She'd spied on them for years, seduced them, used them. She'd helped kidnap Rory, and then she'd tried to kill Quinn. His Quinn. His mate had been scarred for life because of this monster. And now she was back to finish the job? With a shot in the dark as they slept, like the coward she was.

Shayna's eyes went wide as he spun the knife in his grip and brought it toward the side of her neck.

"Dade, stop!" Quinn screamed.

Heaving breath, he halted the blade just shy of slitting Shayna's throat, his weapon faltering on his mission to end this. Quinn was soft and good. If he killed Shayna in front of her, she'd be scared of him. She'd see the grittiest parts of him—the jagged pieces of his broken soul that allowed him to kill to protect the people he loved.

"Listen to your whore," Shayna rasped out.

Dade slammed her against the wall again and glanced back over his shoulder. "Quinn, go downstairs."

"You can't," Quinn whispered, horror in her voice.

"She'll kill you. I can't let her go."

"I know." Quinn lifted the handgun she'd picked up off the floor and aimed it at Shayna's face. "But I can't let you bear the consequences of a kill that is mine to take."

The gun rattled and shook in her trembling grip. His mate was brave, but she wasn't a killer. Not like he was. Pressing his forearm against Shayna's throat, Dade reached back and put his hand over top of the gun. "It's okay, baby. It's okay."

Tears streamed down Quinn's face as she glared at Shayna's blazing silver eyes. "I can see the bear in you. You don't deserve her. You have no honor. All you've done is take without any thought to how your actions affect other people—other shifters. You tried to kill me, and you don't even know me."

"Quinn, you don't want to do this," Dade pleaded. "She'll haunt you."

"Like all of your marks do? Like the innocent targets she helped press you into? More pain because of her."

Dade shook his head slowly and pushed the gun down toward the ground. A sob tore from Quinn as her shoulders sagged. She released the weapon into his grasp and sank to her knees.

A soft, humorless laugh came from Shayna. She spat blood onto the floor and brought her churning mercury eyes to his. "She's already turned you soft."

Dade gave her an empty smile. "You're going to wish I'd killed you quickly, Shayna."

"What the fuck does that mean?"

Dade snatched his cell phone from the dresser beside them and dialed out.

"It means, trust me when I say you would've

rather me exacted a swift vengeance than thrown you to the wolves."

"Hello?" a sleep-filled voice asked into the phone after the first ring.

"Mason?"

"What's happened?"

"Shayna's at my house. Can you send Damon's trackers?"

A beat of silence, then, "Give me ten minutes."

The line went dead, and for the first time ever, Dade saw fear slash through Shayna's eyes.

"Change, Change, Change," Shayna chanted, closing her eyes.

"It's the fear. Do you smell it?" Dade asked, cocking his head as he glared. "You paid someone to put a submissive bear inside of you. Bad buy, Shayna. My animal is meaner and more dominant, thanks to everything you and Krueger put me and my crew through. You won't be able to Change around me. Not unless I allow it."

"Please, Dade. Just let me go." Shayna's voice trembled like a leaf in the wind.

"Too late now," Quinn said from behind him, her voice ringing with hollowness. "The wolves are coming for you."

TEN

Dade stood with his back to her on the front porch as the black SUV drove away. Jeans hung low around his hips as the early morning light glinted off the shiny pink scars on his bare shoulders. His arms were crossed, muscles tensed. He looked like a statue against the coming sunrise.

Quinn's heart ached for him.

Shayna had screamed all kinds of vitriol as he handed her over to a trio of rangy men whose eyes were too bright to be entirely human. She'd taunted him with how IESA had murdered his "worthless father" and how Dade would think of her every time he looked at his "hideous scars" in the mirror. She'd cursed, spat, and told him the only regret she had was not pulling the trigger on Quinn faster so that his soul would be mutilated forever.

Quinn had taken vengeance away from him, and after hearing how much pain that woman had put him through, she honestly didn't know if she'd done the right thing. A man like Dade needed the closure.

A soft apology slipped past her lips. "I didn't want another ghost for you."

His shoulders lifted slightly in a sigh, and he turned his face so she could see his profile. From here, the gold in his eyes was unmistakable. "I know."

Heartbreak filled her chest cavity as she padded across the cold wooden porch planks and slid her hands around his stomach. His abs flexed with every breath under her touch. She rested her cheek against his spine and closed her eyes.

"That gunshot scared me bad, Dade. I thought you were hurt. It's awful to wake up after a night like we had and think everything is over. Think the man you love is gone." She'd already been through that once before, and it had nearly destroyed her. "I know what I can and can't handle, and I can't lose you."

Dade stroked his fingers across her arm and sighed. "You won't." He turned and wrapped her up in a hug that said he'd been shaken up, too. "I promise everything will be okay. I'll make sure of it."

"I think we should go public with what IESA has done to you and your brothers. We can't live our lives thinking people like Shayna will come back and try to tie up loose ends. I think we should go in front of the town, and tell them what has happened. About how you've been treated, so if we go missing, there would be consequences for the agency. There has to be some accountability for IESA."

"That's assuming humans give a shit about what happens to us."

"You're wrong about humans, Dade. Not all of them are bad. And if we want to be a part of society and be accepted, animals and all, we have to be open so that the public doesn't fear us. So that people have a chance to understand us."

"You have so much faith in people."

"Because they deserve a chance. I don't want to wake up always wondering if we're still in one piece. I don't want to live my life thinking you could be taken from me."

Dade's lips crashed onto hers. His tongue drove inside her mouth as a soft whimper escaped her throat. He smelled like fur, and his eyes flashed like fire when he eased back just far enough to lift the T-shirt over her head. "No more talk of losing me, woman. I already told you I'm not going anywhere."

Quinn gasped as he spun her, then pulled her on top of his lap as he sank onto a wooden bench at the edge of the porch. Desperately, she pulled at the button of his jeans and unsheathed his thick cock. It was red and swollen, ready for her, and she yanked the fabric down his thighs.

"You're mine, Dade Leland Keller." She positioned herself over him and slid down, taking him slowly.

Dade bit his lip and rolled his eyes closed as he leaned back on the bench. When she'd taken all of him, she rolled her hips and gripped the back of his hair. His hand kneading her breast, Dade let off the feral sound that said he was barely in control as he pumped his shaft deeper into her, matching her stroke for stroke. He pulled her closer, hugged her tight as the pressure inside of her built to blinding.

"There she is," Dade whispered, stroking her cheeks just under her eyes. "Can you feel her?"

Quinn's insides pulsed with power she'd never

felt before. "Yes," she panted out, rocking against him.

His bear was calling to hers. She could feel him drawing her out, seducing her until a wild growl rattled Quinn's throat. "Oh!" she cried out, closing her eyes against the intensity of her pleasure.

Mindlessly, she leaned forward and sank her teeth into Dade's shoulder until he growled out her name. When she opened her eyes again, her mate wasn't the man she'd been with last night. Gentle Dade was gone, and she reveled in the fact that she'd murdered his control.

Gold eyes blazing, Dade gritted his teeth and stood, then pulled out of her and bent her over the bench on her locked arms. Good bear, doing exactly what her animal wanted.

She threw her head back and cried out his name as he slammed into her from behind. His thick erection drove into her, faster and faster as the growl in her throat rattled until her body vibrated with it. He leaned across her back and cupped her sex where he was entering her, pressed on her clit as he grazed his teeth against her neck.

Faster, deeper, she was gone now, freefalling into nothing. Orgasm crashed through her as Dade swelled and shot jets of warmth into her. Her voice echoed across the clearing as her body pulsed around him. Erratically, Dade bucked into her until he emptied himself completely, filling her until it was too much for her to hold. Slickness trickled down her thighs, and she grinned in triumph as Dade relaxed behind her.

As their breathing slowed, Dade rubbed his fingertips down her ribcage and rocked languidly into her. His lips pressed little random patterns against the sensitive skin of her back, and she gasped softly as she came again.

"You bit me," he whispered as her aftershocks pulsed on.

"You bit me first," she accused through a satisfied smile.

Dade pulled out of her and spun her around, then cupped her cheeks. "To bear shifters, the bite is a way of claiming your mate."

The smile dipped from her face at how serious his voice sounded. "Good," she whispered, gripping his wrists to keep him there. "Then we've claimed each other."

****

"You don't have to be nervous," Dade murmured. He gripped Quinn's thigh and gave her a comforting squeeze before he dragged his gaze back to the road.

"I'm meeting the entire Breck Crew for the first time. Of course, I'm nervous. What happens if they don't like me?"

"First off, it's impossible not to like you, and second, I'd maul anyone who doesn't."

She remembered how graceful and fast he'd been when he'd gone after Shayna this morning with that long, curved knife, and she believed him. It shouldn't have made her feel better that he'd go to such extreme lengths to protect her, but it did, and right now, she didn't really care about what that said about her as a person. She was scared of her future, scared for her mate's future, and her heart hurt as she learned more and more about his past. IESA had created a killing machine, but even with the odds stacked against him, Dade was clinging to his humanity. He could've gone off the rails any time during the years he was being pushed and used and threatened, but he was still here, trying to do what was right—trying to make up for the things he was forced to do by being a firefighter and saving what lives he could.

Proud of the man he was, she pulled Dade's hand to her lips and kissed his knuckles lightly.

His expression softened. "What was that for?"

"I'm just glad your bear picked me. You make me happy."

"Even with everything going on?"

She laughed and shook her head at the craziness that had taken over her life in the past few days. "Even so. You feel worth it."

Dade turned off at a fork in the road. "Look there. Up that road, Cody and Rory live with their cub, Aaron. Boone and I both live off the road we just came down, and Ma and Gage's family live this way."

Another wave of nervous flutters filled her stomach, and she clenched her hands against her thighs. She'd worn a knee length floral dress so her new scars wouldn't be rubbed raw under denim all day, and she'd thrown on a jean jacket and flats to finish off the look. Still, she fidgeted with the light fabric of her dress and hoped it was proper attire for meeting a crew of burly bear shifters for the first time. She'd never been good in crowds, especially if she didn't know anyone, and now they would see how awkward she was. Dade had told her so much about his family she felt like she already knew them. She, on the other hand, was the new bear on the block and also the reason they were dealing with the trauma of coming out to the human public.

"Your heart is racing," Dade murmured as he pulled to a stop in a wild flower field. "You don't have to worry, I promise."

"How do you know?" Her voice came out quivering and weak.

Dade gave her a small, adoring smile, as if she'd amused him. He leaned forward and kissed her, sucking on her bottom lip before he pulled away, and making her feel utterly drunk. "Because...look." He turned his head, and Quinn followed his gaze.

His mother's cabin looked similar in size to his, but with cedar logs around the outside. Colorful patio chairs dotted the porch, and flower pots full of arrangements in every hue of the rainbow hung from rods along the front landscaping. Across the front of the house was a large, hand-painted sign that read *Welcome to the Crew* in blue, yellow, and green lettering.

Out front, a small crowd had gathered, standing

still with expectant smiles on their faces, as if they'd been waiting for her and Dade to arrive.

"Oh," she breathed, pushing her door open. She stood beside the truck, uncertain. "Is that for me?"

"I told you. We don't get new members very often. Come on," he said, holding out his hand. "Ma has been waiting impatiently to meet you."

Behind him, the tall grass of the yard swayed like ocean waves, but Dade stood frozen, waiting. Towering and strong, immovable. Hers.

Quinn slid her palm against his and allowed him to lead her toward the home and the people she would call family someday, if she was lucky enough.

She waved shyly as they approached. It was a silver-haired woman who got to her first with a big genuine smile. "Oh," she drawled, chuckling as she reached for Quinn's shoulders. Pulling her in close, she said, "I never thought my Dade would settle down, and you've done it. You've done it."

Quinn wrapped her arms around the woman's waist and let her rock them. "Why'd you think that, Mrs. Keller?"

"Ma. You'll call me Ma like everyone else." Ma eased back and gripped Quinn's arms, studied her with moisture-rimmed eyes. "Some bears go their whole lives without the need to pair up. I was afraid my boys' animals had been too damaged after everything. You and Rory and Leah have proved that there is hope for them."

"I'm Rory," a fiery red-headed woman said, offering her hand for a shake. "I'm Cody's mate."

Leah, Gage's mate, introduced herself and pulled her into a back-cracking hug like Ma had done. She knew Boone from yesterday, but seeing all the Keller brothers beside each other was intimidating. Cody, with his ice blue eyes and strong chin, Gage with his dark eyes and blond, short hair, easy-smiling Boone with his shoulder length tresses and arm covered in tattoos made him look like a bright-eyed surfer, and Dade—her Dade. All of the Kellers sported the same shade of blond hair and looked similar, but each was different. Different height and build, different demeanors.

Cody and Gage shook her hand one by one, but it was Boone who pulled her in for a rough hug. A trio of towheaded five-year olds ran through the crowd.

"I'm Aaron," the ringleader said in an adorable, squeaky voice. "Me 'n Tate 'n Arie made this for you."

He held up a large sheet of crinkly paper, ripped and bent at the corners, but in the middle was a small herd of what looked like long-clawed bears.

Arie's little pigtails bobbed as she lurched forward and pointed to a bear lying on the ground with its tongue hanging out. "That one's you."

Dade snorted as surprised laughter bubbled from Quinn's throat.

"I'm sorry," Rory said through an apologetic smile. "The kids saw you Change on the television."

"Oh, that's all right," Quinn said, stifling a giggle and taking the picture from Aaron's hands. "It was a rough first Change, so no wonder they drew me like this." It looked like she was being trampled by the other bears. And was that a blood puddle under her head? "It is very good. I'm going to hang it up the second I get home."

With a satisfied nod Aaron exclaimed, "Oh! I also got you this." He handed her a pink paperclip and squeaked out, "Come on!" Then led Tate and Arie on a chase toward a rope swing that hung from a towering pine.

Quinn stared at the little treasure in her hand.

"He has this thing with paperclips," Cody said

through a proud smile as he watched his boy help Arie onto the swing.

Dade rubbed her lower back as she clipped the little gift to the collar of her dress. She would keep always as a memory of the first time she ever laid eyes on the Breck Crew.

"You want a beer?" her mate asked.

"Please." She offered him a grateful smile and followed the Kellers toward the front porch.

"Grab me one, too," Rory called.

"Yep," Dade said. "Leah?"

"Sure, why not?" the dark-headed woman said, bumping Quinn's shoulder. "I think after the week we've had, we could all use a drink."

"About that," Quinn said as she settled into step between Leah and Rory. "I'm really, really sorry about all the trouble I've caused."

"What trouble are you talking about?" Cody asked over his shoulder from up front.

"You know, forcing you to come out to the public."

"Don't blame yourself for that one. No one here does. We were talking about coming out of hiding years before you came along. This was all going to happen eventually. I'd rather you be here for Dade than wait a little while longer."

Quinn swallowed a lump down and wiped her clammy palms against the fabric of her dress. "Thank you for saying that."

"I didn't say it to absolve you," Cody said, turning his honest gaze on her. "This just isn't your fault is all."

Quinn sighed, releasing the weight of a stress she hadn't realized she was carrying. "Thank goodness. I thought you would be mad at me for all of this."

Ma wrapped her arm around Quinn's shoulders and hugged her against her side. "If the blame rests with anyone, it's IESA and that little she-weasel, Shayna, for pushing us into a desperate measure. You just sped up the process, dear. Here, you and Dade can have the glider."

"Thank you," she murmured as she sank onto a lime green two-seat rocker. The clatter of plastic chairs scuttled across the wooden porch floor boards as the others pulled theirs in close. All except Gage who manned a grill on the other side. It smelled like they were making hamburgers, and Quinn's stomach growled in anticipation. "Sorry," she murmured as the Breck Crew turned amused eyes on her. "I can't seem to eat enough since the Change."

"That's not just your bear, Quinn," Ma said as she settled into a rocking chair across from her. She looked pointedly at the red, angry scars that were peeking out from under the hem of Quinn's sundress. "Healing takes it out of you. Gage, when you finish those burgers, can you get Quinn a plate?"

"Yeah, Ma," came his quick answer.

Quinn moved to cover her legs, but Rory reached over from her seat right beside her. "Don't do that. You earned those. This life requires scars. Some are more obvious than others, and some are only on the inside. What matters is how you spend your time during the good parts."

Quinn's eyes burned with tears, and she swallowed hard, determined not to be a complete wuss the first time she met Dade's family.

"Oh, lookey here," Boone crowed. "We've got another sappy bear in the crew. Rory, you aren't alone anymore."

"Shut up," Rory said with a laugh.

Boone wiggled out of swatting range and took a long swig of his beer, still grinning behind the bottle.

"I like her sappy," Dade admitted as he passed Leah and Rory their drinks. He came to a stop in front of Quinn and popped the top of her beer, then handed it to her. "She cares about the things I'd forgotten were important."

"Awwww," Leah said softly. And now she looked all choked up, too.

Boone coughed out the word, "Pussy."

"Tastes delicious," Dade said, sitting beside Quinn, one long leg folded, the other straight, the heel of his heavy boot clomping against the porch. He draped an arm around her, the epitome of male bravado.

"Dade," Quinn gritted out, mortified. Heat rushed to her cheeks at the memory of what he'd done to her right before they'd left the house to come here.

"Boy, I know I raised you better," Ma said, but she was stifling a smile that said she was used to crude antics.

Boone and Dade tinked their beers together as Rory shook her head. From Cody's place leaned against the porch railing where he'd been watching the cubs play, he ducked his head and covered a smile.

Quinn stripped off her jean jacket as her blush upped her internal temperature to Level Magma.

Rory grabbed her arm and traced the bite scar Dade had given her. "Damn, girl. You've been through it lately, haven't you?"

"Yeah, but my girl doesn't stay down for long. Don't let her soft heart fool you. My mate has teeth, and she'll dish it back." Dade tugged the collar of his white T-shirt, exposing the bite mark she'd given him earlier.

Quinn nearly choked on her beer. *Mother effer.* Dade was going to embarrass her to death in front of his ma!

Now, Rory and Leah were clapping slow, talking about how she should've bit him harder, and Boone was trying his damndest to give her a high five she refused. Ma looked surprisingly proud, and Cody was reaching into a blue plastic cooler as he grinned and shook his head.

"Here," the alpha said, just before he tossed her a purple water pistol.

Lurching forward, Quinn barely caught it and gasped as icy water flung onto her bare legs.

"No," Dade said, amused warning in his eyes. "I

was bragging, and it isn't anything to be ashamed of that you like to bite when we're—"

Quinn squirted his chest. "Stop it."

"Making love," he finished, standing to duck out of the way of her shots.

"Dade, stop!"

"Like the bears do!" Dade hooted. "It's natural, baby."

"Shut up!" Damn her stupid unstoppable smile. The man didn't need any encouragement.

Another stream of water came from his left, and Cody grinned maniacally. He didn't have a water pistol like hers. More like a water assault rifle. It was huge. Cody pumped it and blasted Dade again as her mate ducked and ran for the cooler.

There was a split second when Quinn looked at Rory, and they froze, then cracked face-splitting grins, set their beers down in a rush, and ran for the cooler with the others.

Quinn screamed when freezing water blasted against her back as she ran down the porch stairs. She was wielding two matching guns now, but Aaron ran toward her, his little legs moving double-time. "I want to help! I'll protect you!" he called out, and she handed him one of the sloshing weapons. "Uncle Dade, you need to learn better manners!" he yelled, shooting jets of water at her mate as Dade laughed and dodged out of the way.

The tree line looked safe as she fled the water gun fight with Dade and the others on her heels. She sprinted around a tree, laughing uncontrollably as spurts of water barely missed her. She was soaked to the bone, her hair was plastered to her face, and her mascara probably looked like she was crying black rivers, but she couldn't help the throaty laughter coming from her if she tried. The forest was filled with the sound as they ran, weaved, and sprayed each other until even the biggest water soakers were empty.

"Boo," Dade said breathlessly as he leaned around the tree she was hiding behind.

Without thinking, she reached up on her tiptoes and kissed him square on his mouth. He froze in surprise, but relaxed and dropped his plastic weapon with a *thunk*. His arms went around her shoulders, and his lips softened against hers.

When Boone whistled out a catcall and told them to get a room, Dade eased back and told him to "Peel the banana," as he held up his middle three fingers. Then he pulled the outside ones in, flipping his brother off, and Boone said, "Ahh, I see what you did there." Giant water gun slung haphazardly over his shoulder, he strode past them with a wink.

"I like it when you laugh like that," Dade said, quiet as a breath.

"Like a hyena?"

"No, like you mean it. Like you can't help but laugh."

"That was really fun. I thought...well, I thought all of this bear stuff was just going to be really heavy, all the time, every day. I kind of needed a light moment."

Dade's hair was wet and mussed with that sexy, just-got-out-of-the-shower look, and his smile was easier than she'd ever seen it. His defined chest heaved against the nearly transparent white T-shirt she'd soaked, and damn, he was calling to her hormones.

Those whiney hos would have to wait to get banged again, though, because Ma was waving them up to the house for dinner, and she definitely wasn't down with getting busted by Dade's family with her dress up around her hips.

"Squirrel scratch," she said as she wiggled her fingernails against one of his nipples. She bounded off laughing but looked over her shoulder to see him with his hands on his hips, staring down at his one perky bud on that side.

"That's just wrong," he called out. "At least perk up the other one." His voice dipped low. "Preferably with your mouth."

"This bear has teeth, remember?"

Dade scooped her up, and she gasped at how fast he'd gotten to her. "Oh, I remember." He leaned down and kissed her hard, biting her lip at the end, and pulled a little moan from her throat. "It's one of my favorite things about you."

"What's your other favorite things?"

Dade smiled absently at the field they were walking over as he hugged her closer to his chest. "The way you say sweet shit in your sleep."

"I do not. I'm not a sleep talker."

"Says who? You can't hear your own self in your sleep."

"Fine," she said, slipping her arms around his neck. "What did I say?"

"That you loved me."

"Fibber."

"Well, do you?" he asked, blond brows arched high.

She wanted to say no just to argue, but he would hear the lie. "Yes," she murmured, heat creeping up her neck.

"Well," he said, sneaking a glance up at the porch where everyone was lining up to fill their plates. He set her down and gripped her waist with his strong, oversize hands. "Quinn Copeland, I love you back."

Her heart pounded against her ribcage as she searched his dancing eyes. "Dade, don't tease me."

"Wouldn't tease about something like this. I've never said that to a woman before."

She snuggled her cheek against the hard planes of his chest and huffed an emotional sigh.

"Woman, you gonna cry again?"

"No." She *probably* wasn't going to. Looking up into his happy, ocean-colored eyes, she smiled and sighed contentedly as she brushed a damp lock of hair from his forehead. "That's even better than you staying with me for breakfast this morning. Careful, you big scary bear. Keep telling me things like that, and you'll prove Shayna right."

The smile fell from his face slightly as he rocked them side to side in a music-less slow dance. "And how's that?"

"I really will make you soft."

ELEVEN

Dade couldn't stop watching Quinn with Leah and Rory. She sat at the dining room table cutting up with them, looking at old photo albums Ma had dug out. Over the course of the evening, his mate had settled into an easy comfort with them, and wasn't even shying away from conversation anymore.

Ma was humming to herself in the kitchen, washing dishes with Boone. Dade and Cody, meanwhile, were playing wrestle-mania with the cubs. They'd had their baths, and the boys were clad in little matching train pajamas Ma had probably found on sale in town, and Arie was wearing a nightgown with little porcupines printed all over. They smelled like soap and toothpaste and were worked up into a giggling frenzy as he and Cody did fake body slams and choke holds with them.

Aaron rolled him over and pulled on his arm, and Dade tapped out to the delight of Tate, who was clapping and cheering on his cousin. Aaron looked up at him suddenly. The blood drained from his face and his eyes changed to green-gold.

"No, no, no," Dade rushed.

"I don't feel good," Aaron said in a frightened voice, and then a little bear cub exploded from his tiny body.

"Crap," Cody murmured. "It's okay, boy. I've got you." He scooped his furry little son off the ground before he clawed Ma's good rug.

Aaron's little black claws dug into Cody's neck, drawing blood as he hugged onto him, but if Cody felt it, he didn't show it.

Rory half-stood, eyes wide and worried, but Cody gave her a quick peck on the lips and said, "I'm gonna take him out in the woods for a while. We'll be back soon." Absently, he scratched the place behind Aaron's shoulder blades where a huge hump would grow someday when he was a grown grizzly.

"Is he okay?" Quinn asked Rory.

"Yeah, he's fine. He is still getting used to controlling his shifts, though. If you'd believe it, he's actually doing a hundred times better than he was a few weeks ago before I brought him to Cody."

Rory began to explain how she'd raised Aaron on her own for the first part of his life, and Dade swung his attention to Gage's kids. "All right, young 'uns. Time for bed."

"Uncle Daaaade," they whined in unison.

"Uncle Dade is right," Gage said from the couch where he'd been sitting for the better part of an hour trying to fix Ma's ancient landline phone. Gage had already offered to buy her a new one three times tonight, but Ma was the type of lady that grew attached to the things she was used to. She didn't much like change, so Gage had fiddled, and from the curses he muttered under his breath, had failed to fix it.

"Can we stay at grandma's all night?" Arie asked in a pipsqueak voice. Damn, she was a cute kid.

"Up to your mom and dad."

"Can we?" Tate asked, his blue eyes going wide like he already knew how squeeze his parents for what he wanted.

"Fine with me," Ma called from the kitchen. "I've got some banana pancake mix I need those kids to help me make in the morning." She gave Leah a wink.

"I'll bet they are more trouble than help in the kitchen, but its fine with me if they stay. We can pick them up first thing in the morning." Leah flipped open a new photo album and frowned. "Ma, I didn't know you made one of these for Bruiser."

Ma rinsed a plate, set it on the drying rack, dried her hands on a towel, and sauntered into the dining area to look. "Of course I have an album for him. I made one for all my boys."

Dade stood and lifted Gage's twins with him, tickling them with his facial scruff. "Night, baby bears."

Arie cupped his face and looked somber as she gave him a slow-motion blink. "Goodnight, Uncle Dade."

He tried to hide the dumb smile splitting his face at how friggin' adorable his niece and nephew were. Setting them down, he patted them on the rumps and sent them scampering into the bed Ma had set up for her grandkids to spend the night, yelling their goodbyes to the rest of the crew as they went.

Curiosity never killed a bear as far as he knew, so he ambled on into the dining room and leaned on locked arms against the table beside his mate. She rested her head against his elbow, just about bringing him to his knees with how damned cute she was.

Maybe she was right. Perhaps he really was going soft.

Kissing the top of her head, he squinted at the pictures.

"Who's Bruiser?" Quinn asked.

"He's my half-brother."

Quinn lifted a surprised glance to Ma. "Oh, I didn't realize there were more in the crew."

"Oh, he's not in our crew. Not anymore. He had a calling somewhere else and joined up with the Ashe Crew in Montana." Ma swung a dreamy look to a black and white photo of Bruiser sitting in a poppy field next to an old hound dog that used to run wild around the property. "I talked to him this morning on the phone, and he asked if we needed him here. Said he would bring Diem and come up here to support us going public if we wanted. I told him to hold off getting those plane tickets until things settle down, though. It's one thing if he comes out with us, but his mate is a different kind of shifter. I don't think she should be anywhere around this situation, and I bet her daddy would agree."

"Good call," Boone rumbled, settling into a chair across the table. "Finding out bear shifters exist is one thing. Finding out a dragon shifter exists is a whole different can of worms."

"Dragon shifter?" Quinn asked, petal pink lips opening slightly with shock. Damn, he wanted to kiss the surprise from her mouth.

"Yeah," Leah said with a knowing look. "I freaked out when I heard that, too. I had no idea they still existed, and Bruiser married one."

"Is she scary?"

"Woman," Boone said with a frown at Quinn, "you had a water gun fight with a bunch of fully mature grizzly shifters, and you haven't batted an eyelash all night. I know you aren't a scaredy bear."

"Yeah, but it's easy to forget you have a bear in you. I almost forget I have a bear in me sometimes. But dragons?"

"I've talked to Diem on the phone a couple of times," Rory said, turning to another picture of Bruiser, this one of him on his first day of eighth grade, holding up his year sign in front of the cabin they used to live in. "She sounds really nice. And she seems to really love Bruiser. I'm excited about them visiting when everything settles down."

Gage turned on the television in the living room, probably to catch the evening news.

Quinn grinned and said "awww" at a picture in Dade's book of him in a pair of tighty whiteys and Dad's oversize work boots. He was probably five there.

"Oh, geez," he muttered.

"Hey, guys?" Gage said softly. "Come in here. You've got to see this."

Dade took Quinn's hand and helped her out of the chair, then led her into the living room. He pulled her onto his lap on the couch beside his oldest brother and rested his hands across the scars on her thighs.

No one said a word as the story panned to protestors holding signs that declared the government needed to regulate shifter lives, or imprison them, or separate them from the human population. It made him ill to see the signs with Xs over pictures of bears. One sign read *Hunting Season*

Has Begun, and Dade held Quinn a little closer. He'd die before he let anyone hurt her, or any of the rest of his family.

The local news reporter stood in front of the crowd, talking about how long the protests had gone on, but she looked uncomfortable with the story and fumbled the words. "Just a few short days ago, the world was rocked with the emergence of a strain of supernatural creatures. Bear shifters are real, the proof in the transformation of this woman on camera, as well as the family of shifters who turned her."

Quinn's name and picture flashed across the screen. Even in this shot, she looked uncomfortable in front of the camera, as if she had shied away from whomever had taken the picture.

Sitting up straight and rigid in his lap, Quinn went pale and her gray eyes round as she whispered, "That's my driver's license picture. On television." Some people might enjoy their fifteen seconds of fame, but his mate was not one of them. She looked like she wanted to bolt and hide.

He rubbed her back until her picture disappeared from the screen.

"I know her," Boone said, gesturing to the

reporter who was describing Quinn's Change by the burning vet clinic. "She was there when you Turned Quinn. She was the one who told us to stop answering questions."

"That's Cora Wright," Leah said. "She does the local news around here. Her covering this story would get her national attention, though."

Clutching her microphone until her knuckles went white, Cora said, "We've seen how emotional it is up here in Colorado where residents are scared of the unknown. The fact is, there is just so little knowledge on these people that no one can determine if they are a threat or if they are as harmless as any other neighbor." Cora covered an ear piece on one side and frowned, as if she heard something she didn't agree with. A frustrated huff left her lips as she pulled the piece from her ear and tossed it to her camera man. "I don't know much about them, but I was there when they came out of hiding. When they Changed for the world to see, and I can tell you my own personal perception of what happened. If you turn down the volume on the screaming and terror on those videos, you'd see a close-knit family group who saved a woman's life.

Who didn't charge or hurt anyone, even though one of their own was shot by some trigger-happy idiot with a gun. By my count, they hurt exactly zero people that day, but managed to save a woman's life. And the shifter who had been shot went beyond the call of his honorable job and stood over her body as if he was protecting her at the risk to his own life. These are men who have served our country—don't you turn that camera off, Carl—ignore them. These are men who have served our country and our communities. In Breckenridge and the surrounding area, they have helped put out house fires, forest fires, they've gone in when buildings were collapsing to save people who were trapped. That doesn't sound like a dangerous wild animal to me. How many of you could say you'd do that? Put your life on the line every day for people who treat you like this." She swung her arm back toward the protesters who were chanting, "Cage them all!"

"You there!" she called, crooking her finger. "Would you like to tell me why you are supportive of the bears?"

Four little old ladies with blue hair bustled in front of the camera.

"That's Aunt Leona," Rory said on a shocked breath.

Dade smiled at the thought that Breckenridge's own Blue-Haired Ladies were their champions.

"I've watched you out here, rallying people for the protection of shifters. I'd like to hear your thoughts on what has happened here this week."

Aunt Leona pulled the microphone to her painted lips and shoved her glasses farther up her nose with determination as the other Blue-Haired Ladies formed a wall blocking the camera from the protestors in the background. "I'm here because my niece Rory is a good girl. And since their names have all been leaked to the public, her five-year-old little boy has been threatened, and her mate has been shamed, and for what? Because they are different. My Rory is a wonderful mother, worried about her family, and her mate has treated her like a queen. He treats everyone with the utmost respect. Here," she said, handing the reporter a printed pamphlet. "I've talked to Rory, and here are some facts about what they are, who they are, and some of the challenges they are facing with this news going public. Protesting something, or someone, just because they

183

are different is *wrong*. They are kind, caring people who do so much for their community. And I and the other Blue-Haired Ladies are calling for an emergency town meeting to discuss this new information about these people who have been a part of our town for three generations. They deserve to at least have the chance to answer our questions. Then we can decide if they are a threat or not. Which they aren't, and the people behind me are being butt-faced, ninny-lickin', twit-wagon—"

Doris Leach, one of the Blue-Haired Ladies, reached from behind Aunt Leona and clamped her hand over her friend's mouth. "Town meeting. That's what we want!"

Cora turned her serious gaze to the camera. "You've heard it straight from the mouths of some of Breckenridge's most prominent members. Town meeting, and we can settle the rage that is humming in our streets tonight. This is Cora Wright saying give the shifters a chance to explain themselves before you damn an entire culture. Thank you and goodnight."

The screen switched to a weatherman in front of a screen, wide-eyed as if he hadn't expected Cora to go off the rails like that. He stuttered and stumbled over his words as he tried to predict a storm that was supposed to blow through tonight.

Gage clicked off the television and shook his head. He looked as sick as Dade felt.

"Rory, was what she said true?" Leah asked. "Has Aaron been threatened?"

Rory suddenly looked exhausted as she nodded slowly. "We all have. Cody's been fielding phone calls left and right, trying to put out fires as they start, but most of it is just awful. He turned off his phone tonight just to get a break from it. He wanted the family to have a good night and for us to celebrate Quinn's induction into our crew without worrying about what is happening out there."

Quinn's hands were shaking, so Dade placed his over hers in a silent promise that he would make everything okay.

"I think," Quinn whispered, "we should say yes if they ask us to attend a town meeting and answer questions. People are afraid because they don't understand you...us." She inhaled deeply and looked shaken to her core. "If we can, I think we should be open with the public and put a stop to the rumors that are probably hurting any chance of us having a normal future."

"She's right," Cody said from the doorway.

Aaron was cradled against his chest, and Rory stood with a blanket to cover her sleepy boy.

"I've talked to every crew we know of, and most of them are pissed, but that doesn't change the fact that this could get worse and worse if we don't cooperate. The Ashe Crew has thrown in their full support, along with the Boarlanders, Gray Backs, and twelve other crews across the country. They are willing to come out to the public if we can't handle this alone. Safety in numbers and all. I'd rather it not get that far, though. My guess is that the government will make us register as shifters, but this was our choice, and the right to come out or not should be up to each individual crew. As of now, we're on our own. I'll call Cora Wright and see if she'll cover our story. She seems like a shifter sympathizer who could be a good asset to us. I'll start putting it in motion we are willing to attend the town meeting. Be aware it will gain national attention, though, so you'll all have to be perfect. Not just okay, but relatable. The public has to feel safe around us."

Dade inhaled deeply and nodded. "I say yes."

"Yeah," Gage said lifting his finger.

"Looks like we're doing this," Boone said, arms over his chest as if he'd do this shit, but wouldn't like it.

The women nodded one by one.

"Okay, I'll make the calls. Monroe has upped security around our property for tonight but be wary. Shayna slipped past them easy enough."

"Shayna?" Rory asked in a horrified voice. "I thought she was in the wind."

Now, she was probably in a shallow grave somewhere, but Dade wasn't going to say that little gem out loud. Quinn had enough to deal with without Shayna's demise on her mind. Damon Daye had called him earlier, and all he'd said was, "It is done."

"You don't have to worry about Shayna coming after you anymore, Rory. She won't be hurting you or Quinn or anyone else." Dade leveled Cody's mate with a serious gaze and hoped she understood what he was really saying when he murmured, "She's not a threat anymore."

"Okay," Rory whispered, shrinking back against Cody.

"Everyone get some rest tonight," Cody said, authority in his words cracking against the quiet house. "Tomorrow, we take our lives back."

TWELVE

"Are you okay?" Dade asked as he rubbed her leg and leveled her with a worried look.

Quinn swallowed her heaving breath and looked around the busy entrance to town hall. It seemed like the entire state of Colorado was outside, picketing or cheering, though she couldn't figure out who was winning.

"Hey," he said softly, turning down the country song that was playing on the radio. "You don't even have to talk today. Cody just wants the entire crew there for moral support. Me and my brothers will handle all the questions, and you can just sit with Rory, Ma, and Leah."

"And the cubs." That was the part that worried

189

her. The cubs would be subject to all of this chaos, and her bear got riled up just thinking about those little kiddos being in danger.

"Yeah," he said, nodding slightly. "And the cubs. Quinn."

"Hmm?" She arced her gaze away from the crowd that was ten seconds away from rocking the truck.

"I love you."

The world melted away as she drowned in his slow smile. "I love you, too."

"We're going to be okay."

A tremendous crash sounded, and window glass shattered inward. Quinn screamed as Dade shielded her with his body.

Quinn looked past Dade's shoulder in shock as a man carrying a large rock was pushed back from the pickup by police.

"Go, go, go!" Monroe yelled, and Dade eased onto the gas and maneuvered through the crowd behind Mason's SUV that was carrying the rest of the crew.

They were packed in there so tightly there hadn't been room for her and Dade.

He drove through a security barricade that was

opened for them and put the truck in park.

"Will it be safe here?" she asked. Dade loved his ride.

"It'll be fine as long as the police are able to hold the protestors back. Come on. Let's get inside so it can settle down out here."

"I don't understand," she said as he helped her from the truck. "Why is everyone so angry? We haven't done anything to them."

"Because they don't understand us. People fear what they don't understand, and for humans, fear manifests as anger." He jerked his head toward the protestors behind them. "The pack mentality here isn't helping either."

News crews were lined up along the steps, tossing out questions left and right. Quinn couldn't begin to answer one before another one was asked, and she became overwhelmed under the blinding flashes of the cameras. Her instincts to flee buzzed constantly, and it was all she could do not to give into her inner animal, turn tail, and run back for the truck.

When she looked up, Dade's eyes were a bright gold, his attention only for the door as he guided her past the throng of photographers. He looked so sure of himself, so stoic and immoveable. If she didn't know what the inhuman color of his eyes meant, she would've thought him completely unaffected by the chaos around them.

One step through the door brought relief as her eyes landed on the rest of the Breck Crew who were waiting in the hallway for them. Rory's wide green eyes made her look as overwhelmed as Quinn felt.

"What happened?" Boone asked, brushing her hair away from a stinging gash on the side of her face.

"They broke our window," she uttered on a breath. "They just broke it...with a big rock."

Ma pulled a package of tissues from her purse and began to dab her face, but Dade had been the one to take the brunt of the shattering glass. His neck was cut in several different places, and red swelled in little droplets against his cheek. "Ma, can you clean Dade up? I'm just going to fix myself up in the bathroom."

"Of course. Rory, you go with her and make sure she is all right. Hurry, though. We only have ten minutes before we have to be in there."

"I don't want you away from me right now," Dade said low.

How did she explain she was scared to death and needed a minute to calm her nerves in a bathroom stall? He'd think she was weak, and Dade deserved better. He deserved a strong mate. "The bathroom is right here," she said pointing to the sign to their left. "Wait for me."

Dade lifted his lip in a snarl, and a rumbling growl filled the space between them. "Come back to me quick."

With a nod, Quinn bustled into the bathroom with Rory trailing. The mirror was one judgmental little skank. Quinn glared at her pallid reflection and colorless lips. The cut on her temple was already closing, but a smear of red remained. Thank heavens for bear shifter healing. Damp paper towel in hand, she washed her face gently, careful not to scrape off the heavy layer of make-up she'd slathered on to try to cover how scared she was. Apparently, that stupid plan wasn't working.

"Here, let me," Rory murmured. "You're getting your hair all damp." She snatched the cloth from Quinn's hand and made quick work of fixing the damage. Then she rifled through her purse, handed Quinn a tube of pink lip gloss, and quickly combed the snarls from Quinn's wavy tresses with practiced fingers. When she was satisfied, she turned to her own reflection and let off a frustrated sound.

Quinn bounded into a bathroom stall and shut the door behind her. She was breathing so fast she was going to pass out, and then what use would she be to the Breck Crew? She wouldn't even be good moral support.

"You can do this," she whispered to herself, wishing she'd figured out how to handle people staring at her when she'd taken a public speaking class in college. All she'd learned was that she could do worse by the end of the semester than in the beginning. She'd nearly peed her pants during the final, and in front of the entire lecture hall, then walked out halfway through her terribly enunciated speech on the use of technological devices in education. Her teacher had given her a C, probably so she wouldn't retake the class. That, or she took pity because she thought Quinn was having a medical meltdown in front of everyone.

"Quinn? Are you all right?" Rory asked.

She took a steadying breath and opened the door, averting her eyes to hide her panic.

"Oooh." Rory waved her hand around Quinn's face. "You look like a bear."

Quinn glanced at her reflection in the mirror and groaned. Well, now she and Dade could match monster eyes. "This is going to go awesome," she said sarcastically.

"That's the spirit," Rory muttered, shoving her toward the door.

Dade waited with his hands behind his back, a formal gesture she'd never seen him do before. He looked sexy in his dark dress pants and blue button-up. His eyes seemed even brighter near the color of that fabric.

Onlookers were crowded in the hallway, but they were a different breed than the protestors outside. If they hated them, they showed it with dirty looks and whisper instead of rocks and hate-signage.

The Blue-Haired Ladies were there, talking to Cody and Rory, and bobbing their heads with the seriousness of whatever discussion they were entombed in.

"Quinn!" Dr. Voss called from down a hallway as they walked by. "Oh, good, I thought you'd go in before I caught you." The vet took her hands in her own and squeezed them comfortingly. "I just wanted you to know you'll have a friendly face in there."

Relief flowed through Quinn, allowing her tense shoulders to relax by millimeters. "It's so good to see you. I'm so sorry about your clinic."

"Don't be. We'll rebuild with what insurance is giving us. It's a frustrating inconvenience, but the important thing is that no one was hurt. I'm so glad you made it out of there." Dr. Voss leaned closer. "And I'm so glad it was Dade and those Keller boys who found you. I'll call you when the clinic re-opens and you can start right where you left off. No matter what happens today, you'll have a job at my clinic if you want it."

"Really?"

"Yes, of course." Dr. Voss pointed to her chest. "Animal advocate, remember?"

"Oh, right." Because she was part animal now. *Still really weird to think about.* Quinn gave her a grateful smile and thanked her, then she and Dade bustled after the rest of the Breck Crew.

The exchange with Dr. Voss made her feel better. Not all humans would accept them, but some would. Some were good and understanding and accepting—

like the Blue-Haired Ladies and the group of bystanders near the window who *weren't* shooting death lasers at her with their eyes. And Dr. Voss. And Moira. As Quinn passed, she waved to the doctor, dressed in a coral business suit and nude pumps.

Quinn's high heels echoed off the tile floors, and as she came to a stop with the rest of her crew in front of towering double doors, she smoothed the wrinkles form her mint green dress. All she had to do was sit in there next to Rory and show her solidarity. This wasn't so bad. It was cake—if she could forget all the cameras trained on her.

The seats were filling up inside the sprawling room, and the volume of murmuring increased the second Cody walked across the threshold. Dade's strong hand on her lower back was the only thing keeping her knees from buckling against the forward movement.

Cody led the crew to a long table up front, angled to face both the large room and a similar table where seven older men and women sat. If the name plates were anything to go by, it was the mayor and town council members.

She took a seat between Dade and Rory, who

was cuddling Aaron close in her lap.

"Good evening," Mayor Randolph said in a booming, authoritative voice that silenced the crowd as they took their seats in rows of plastic chairs. "We are here tonight to speak candidly with a new and emerging group of people who are members of our town. The decision on what to do about them is ultimately up to our great government, but as for this meeting, we can open up lines of communication and begin to understand one another so that we can assure you that Breckenridge is still a safe place to live." Mayor Randolph's dark hair shone in the fluorescent lighting as he turned his steely gray eyes on Cody. "Our main concern is all of the negative attention we are receiving in the media. As you know, this is a town that thrives on tourism. If the tourism isn't there for us, we lose jobs, residents, and funding for schools."

"That's bull-honkey and you know it," Rory's Aunt Leona spoke up. "I call it now. This skiing season will be the best one yet. Everyone will flock here to try to get a glimpse of the bear shifters. Already, two of the condos are booked through the entire winter and into spring."

Mayor Randolph narrowed his eyes. "In an attempt to keep some semblance of order today, I'll ask that you refrain from speaking until asked to do so."

Aunt Leona glared but sat down beside the other Blue-Haired Ladies and zipped her lips.

"Great," Randolph muttered. "Now, I think we should start this meeting with the shifters introducing themselves and giving us a brief history of their kind."

Cody cleared his throat and nodded, then stood and addressed the room. "My name is Cody Keller. Some of you know me as one of the town firefighters, along with my brothers, Gage,"—he pointed—"Boone, and Dade. We are third generation firefighters. Some of you knew our father, Titus Keller, who presumably died fighting a fire right inside city limits when I was fifteen. This is my mate, Rory, and our son Aaron. Rory is human. Aaron is like me."

"Why do you call her your mate instead of your wife?" a woman in a purple dress asked.

Mayor Randolph looked annoyed, but allowed it.

"Marriage is a human tradition that we only

sometimes participate in. For us, pairing up and claiming a mate is the equivalent of marriage. We bond with one mate for life. The rate of infidelity for bear shifters is almost none because our animals simply won't allow it."

"But bears in real life mate with several partners."

"Yes, true, but we don't. It's not how we are wired," Cody explained.

"But you'll still spit on the sanctity of marriage and raise families never being married," the woman in the purple dress called out.

"Ma'am, with all due respect, there are lots of people in this society who aren't allowed to get married, but that doesn't mean they aren't a family. Rory and Aaron are my family. Gage is mated to Leah, and they have twin cubs, and they are a family. We aren't aiming to smite out marriage, and in fact, Rory and I are planning a ceremony in the winter to bind us legally. But it isn't necessary for us. It's just a different culture. Being mated is equivalent to being married. My brother Dade is a prime example of it. Dade?"

Dade slid his hand off Quinn's thigh and stood.

"Some bear shifters go their entire lives without the urge to settle on one mate, and then some of us are lucky enough to form a bond. In Rory and Quinn's case, they were both human when Cody and I fell for them, so it isn't dependent on them also being shifters. For Leah, however, she was born a bear shifter, and Gage knew instantly they were it for each other. For our kind, it works very fast. It's a very powerful motivator to want to please our mates because their happiness allows us to be happy. It's like...first love, but all those months it takes to form that bond wrapped up into an instant. With Quinn, I knew the second I set eyes on her she was mine."

"And what if the woman doesn't want you back? What then? Does your animal side force them?" a man called out.

"Absolutely not," Boone said, standing. "Women in our culture are revered and make their own decisions. If they don't feel the bond, it's their choice to tell us to fuck off."

"Language," Cody warned.

"Can the infection spread through sex with the human population?" one of the council members asked.

Rory stood and held Aaron tightly. "I'm Cody's mate. He is a very dominant bear shifter, and the alpha of what we call our crew. I can assure you, I'm still very much human and will remain so until I choose to Turn. Which might be never because I don't envy what they have to go through."

"Like what?" Mayor Randolph asked.

"Like the pain of the Change is very real. I watched my son experience it for years before I came back here seeking help from Cody and his Breck Crew. It is something I wouldn't wish on anyone. In addition to that, our crew has been taken advantage of by a special interest group called IESA. The men in our crew have been forced to do many, many things they didn't want to because they were threatened with exposure, death, and the torture of their families. Which is why we have decided to come out to you and beg for your aid to stop the exploitation of our kind. We are just trying to live our lives quietly, but many of our kind have been killed simply for not doing missions IESA ordered them to."

"Have you killed anyone?" a man asked in a hard voice.

"No," Rory said, anger flashing across her green

eyes.

"Not you, human. I'm talking to the bear shifters."

"They served their country in wartime," Rory gritted out. "That isn't a fair question."

"If a human is going to speak for them, why are we even here?" the man asked, his bald dome shining with sweat.

"Answer the question," Mayor Randolph said.

"Don't," Cora Wright ordered from beside a camera man. She held a microphone in one hand and a notepad scribbled with notes in the other. "You don't have to answer anything without a lawyer and a trial. You aren't being accused of anything today. This is a question and answer meeting only, not a trap to string you up." She narrowed her eyes at the sneering man. "Next question."

"No answer means yes!" the man yelled. "They've murdered people. Humans. And we're just going to let murderers live unpunished in our town. Fuck that."

Quinn shook her head as the crowd erupted. It wasn't fair. Most of the people the Kellers had killed were shifters at the order of IESA.

"What kind of shifters are there?" an older woman asked over the erupting crowd.

Looking troubled, Cody stood and leaned toward a microphone. "That we can't tell you since we aren't sure. It wouldn't be our place to talk about people who have nothing to do with us."

"How can we be sure our children would be safe around your children in a public school system?"

"Because we teach them to behave just the same as you teach yours to."

"Mine don't have teeth and claws. They don't have built in weapons! I want any shifter cub, as you call them, registered as a shifter, wearing a name badge or tracking bracelet or something so that we can easily identify what and where they are."

Panic seized Quinn's throat at the thought of how close they were getting already to discussing trackers. Dade swallowed hard beside her and shot her a wide-eyed look. They were losing control of this meeting.

"Are males the only bear shifters able to Turn humans?"

"No," Cody said, shaking his head.

"Are you trying to take over the world?" a man

shouted.

"What? No," Cody growled out.

"Quiet down!" Mayor Randolph warned.

"Is the Breck Crew a cult?"

"Why have you decided to come out now?"

"Do you eat raw meat, more specifically human flesh when you are in your animal form?"

"How fast can you heal?"

"Maybe if we put them in special housing behind fences..."

"Do you live forever like vampires?"

"How many of you are there?"

Cody sat heavily into his chair, looking at Rory as if he were utterly overwhelmed.

"Enough!" Quinn screamed, standing so fast her chair clattered to the floor behind her.

"Introduce yourself," Cora called out in a rush.

The room dipped to silence.

Quinn's voice quivered, and her breath shook. "I'm Quinn Copeland, the one you saw on that awful video. I was human a few days ago, and now I'm not."

"Babe, you don't have to do this," Dade whispered, worry pooling in his sea green eyes.

"I do," she said, gulping down a sob and glaring

at the audience. She clenched her trembling hands at her sides and lifted her voice. "I can't just sit here and watch you all pick apart a group of people who are more amazing than you can imagine. You have mentioned putting tracking bracelets on them, on their cubs, but here is what you haven't considered. That's already been done. Dade, please stand up."

With an uncertain glance at the crowd, he did.

"This is my mate." Dammit she was already getting choked up just thinking about doing this. "I met him before the fire, and he tried to stay away from me because of this." She tugged his top button loose and pointed to the horrific chemical burn that spread across his throat. Several audience members gasped and murmured, but she pressed on. "He wanted to keep me safe from what IESA was doing to them under the radar of the public's attention. This burn was caused by a tracker that IESA had placed in his neck, as well as every bear shifter here, including those two little babies over there, Tate and Arie. They wanted to put one in Aaron, too, and that's when Cody made the decision to make a stand. If it were you or your children, would you submit to having trackers surgically implanted in your necks? To be controlled by the threat of a kill switch? IESA detonated my mate's tracker, and acid did this. His father was killed the same way, though it was made to look like an accident to the public. Countless other shifters have been killed using these techniques and others like them, and the worst part? *These people aren't dangerous to you.* I don't want to hear anything more about trackers. Cody's hand was ruined trying to dig that damned thing out of Dade's neck before IESA pushed that kill switch on him. You ask if they've killed people, but you were the ones who threw them a parade when they came home from war, both times. My mate bears the deep scars of fighting for his country and serving his community, and he's never once complained. He's a good man."

"He isn't a man!" Baldy yelled.

"He *is* a man! And I'm a woman, and these three precious angels are children. I am new to the Breck Crew, but I can tell you my experience with them as a human and as a shifter. They're kind and close-knit. They love each other and have a strong moral compass. They worry about their children's future above their own safety." The first tear slipped down her cheek as she looked at the people she adored.

Rory was crying, and she gripped her hand and held it tight. "I can tell you they are good, honest people who have been through so much just trying to survive, and they are still fighting to remain servants to their community and to people in need, if you'll let them. IESA wasn't going to stop pressing on them until they were all dead. This is a group of people striving to be treated with dignity, trusting humans who call us monsters, and begging for the help of the public. We aren't here to take over the world, nor can I even imagine them Turning anyone they hadn't chosen as a mate. It's against the rules of their culture." She looked up at Dade beside her. "Of *our* culture. And I'm scared," she admitted, swinging her beseeching gaze to the quiet room. "I've only just learned bear shifters existed like you have. I understand your fear, but I'm standing in front of you, telling you that these people are incredible. I haven't really had a family before, and now I feel like I'm right where I'm supposed to be with people who genuinely care about me. Which is crazy because I have a freaking bear inside of me. I'm scared to death of my first conscious Change, and I'm scared I won't be any good at this. And I'm definitely scared of public speaking and the insane amount of attention this has garnered. And those cameras over there are super-duper terrifying."

A few soft chuckles sounded from the crowd, and she laughed thickly and wiped her damp lashes with her knuckles.

"But mostly, I'm scared of something bad happening to my family. They are the reason I'm here, still breathing, still living. I fell in love with this incredible man, but the scars on his body say there will always be a chance something bad will happen to him if we can't find a way to fit into society without being exploited. These people, these bear shifters, are just like you in so many ways. They laugh and tell dirty jokes. They're loyal and have water gun fights and barbecues. They go to their jobs and take pride in their work. They love their families without abandon. Without a single question of distrust, they accepted me into their crew and are helping me through this transition with such tender attention and affection. And I know this won't change some of your minds. You'll hang onto your hate because you think this world is only big enough for humans. I'm sorry for it, but it isn't in my power to change every mind. I just hope that some of you will consider that we aren't the monsters you thought we were. We're just men and women and children who have to turn into a bear for a few hours every couple of weeks. We're just people who are tired of hiding."

Someone began clapping slowly in the audience, and another followed. More joined in until the sound of applause was deafening. Some walked out, and some looked angry, but the cheering overwhelmed the jeering. Cora Wright nodded her head slowly as she clapped, eyes on Quinn with something akin to pride in her eyes. The Blue-Haired Ladies in the front were whistling and cheering, and Moira stood leaned against a side wall, a smile stretching her face. Even Mayor Randolph was clapping.

And when she looked toward the door, a man with dark hair and sparking gold-green eyes stood stoically. The corners of his lips turned up in a slow smile. He offered her a small wave and mouthed *well done*. She recognized him from the photo albums Ma had showed her. Bruiser Keller had come to show his support after all.

And from the way Ma was sobbing with her hands over her mouth at the end of the row, her shoulders shaking with emotion and her eyes locked on Bruiser, she'd seen her adopted son, too.

Rory squeezed her hand even tighter as tears streamed down her face, matching Quinn's.

And Dade. Her Dade. Her tall, confident, steadfast mate was staring at her with such adoration in his eyes. He blinked hard and cupped her cheek. "You're amazing," he whispered, and she glowed under his tender touch and hushed compliment.

Leaning forward, he pressed his lips against hers, settling the rest of the remaining nerves that fluttered around in her stomach.

Easing back, Dade rested his forehead against hers. She closed her eyes and inhaled his scent as the pad of his thumb traced little circles across her cheek.

For as long as she lived, she was in this with him.

He'd saved her life, then given her so much more. Her bear, love, friendship, a family. A home.

From now on, no more hiding. No more fear.

For the rest of always, she would stand tall beside her crew in the arms of the man who had proved worthy of her heart.

EPILOGUE

"You can do this. Just open yourself up to her," Dade advised.

He sat on the porch cuddling two very happy-looking doggies in his arms. Daffodil and Beans now followed Dade wherever he went. Arms tingling with nervousness, Quinn jumped up and down in front of Dade's cabin, naked as a jaybird and covered in gooseflesh from the chilly wind.

She snorted a laugh as Dade bent down and kissed one of the pink bows on top of Daffodil's head. He didn't have a shirt on, and his scars stood stark all over his body. His eyes were bright because he was on the verge of needing to Change, but that didn't stop him from cuddling the frilliest dogs on the planet.

"I can't even take your advice seriously with you cuddling those dogs like that. Big tough guy. Just a werebear and his yorkies."

"Bear shifter," he corrected. He set them down and herded them inside.

Her dogs listened to Dade way better than they did to her. If she told them to go inside like that, they'd look at her like she needed to make them bacon first.

"I only get to play with Tank when I work my forty-eight hour shifts, woman. In between, I get time with Daffodil and Beans."

She snorted a laugh at their ridiculous names in his deep baritone voice.

"Now stop messing around and focus. You were the one who wanted to Change today."

"Yeah, because Bruiser is Changing with everyone else, and it's hard for all of us to get together. I don't want to be left out."

"Well, Bruiser has a flight to catch. He's missing Diem and needs to get back to the Ashe Crew, so chop chop. They're probably all waiting on us."

"You're rushing me."

Dade hooked his hands on his hips and arched his brows. "I told you I'd draw your bear from you, and you said you didn't want the help."

"I'm scared."

He sighed, tossing his head back and glaring at the lone rain cloud above. "Then let me do it for you this first time, and you won't have to be scared anymore." He settled his gold gaze back on her. "Deal?"

"I got a sticker in my foot." She plucked the little thorn from her arch and pouted. Not because it really hurt, but because it was funny watching Dade shake his head with an utter look of defeat.

He gritted his teeth and pulled her waist against him, then kissed her hard, tongue pushing past her lips and brushing hers. A soft moan wrenched from her throat as she slid her hands up his chest and around his neck.

He rolled his hips against her, his denim brushing her sex. He bit her bottom lip and pulled on the backs of her knees until she encircled his hips.

A soft growl rattled her chest, and she eased back, feeling her animal stretch awake inside of her. "Oooh, I see what you did there."

"Well, don't fight her, woman. Let her out."

Her breath sped up as panic constricted her throat at the thought of becoming *other*. But if she wanted to join the rest of the Breck Crew today to celebrate Bruiser's visit, along with their small victory in the news, she had to let this happen.

"Do you trust me?" Dade whispered.

Quinn nodded. "Always."

He set her down and shucked his jeans. And with a cocky, crooked smile that she adored, he arched back and yelled. His voice turned into a deep roar as a dark-furred grizzly burst from him. The earth shook as he landed on all fours in front of her. Powerful legs and a big barrel chest. Long, curved canines and paws the size of her head. His neck was thickly muscled, and his eyes were still that green-gold that all of the Kellers possessed. He was magnificent.

With a proud smile, she watched him saunter a few steps toward the tree line, then look back at her over his shoulder, waiting.

The tingling in her arms spread through her chest, and she cried out in surprise as a smattering of cracks shook her body. One more breath, and she closed her eyes against a blast of power that shook her entire body to its core.

Blood humming, she rocked forward and stared in awe at her six-inch black claws that dug divots in the earth. Her fur was dark as a redwood, and when she tried to speak, a soft, feral grunt filled her throat.

Dade rubbed his face down hers, then down her side. The last of the tingling sensation faded as he inhaled her fur and snuffled against her neck. She'd been so scared of this, and for what? Dade was here. She was safe. And—she looked down at her paws, covered in weapons—being a bear was awesome.

Her whole life, she'd felt an affinity with animals, and now she was one.

She inhaled the earthy scent of the surrounding woods, committing them to memory as home. As a reward for his patience, she play bit Dade's thick neck and rubbed her head under his chin. He let off a huffing sound like a laugh.

Come on, he seemed to say as he tilted his head toward a trail that cut through the trees. Quinn walked close beside him through their woods.

And as the feral call of the Breck Crew filled the air, she hurried her steps, eager to see them.

Brushing her head against Dade's thick fur once

more, she charged forward, her feet pounding the earth as her heart raced with happiness.

These woods were home, and the roaring bears calling her to them were family.

No matter what the fates had in store for her crew, no one could take this away from her.

She had everything.

Sneak Peek

Bear the Heat

(Fire Bears, Book 3)

Chapter One

A thunderous booming sounded against the walls of Boone Keller's cabin. Muscles jerking, he sat up in bed. The pounding rattled his front door a second time, and he lurched for the bedroom light switch. The illumination burned his eyes, and he winced and shielded his face from the harsh lights above.

The knocking was louder now, and if the person on the other side of that door didn't quit, they were going to splinter the wooden barrier that stood between him and the woods outside.

"I'm coming," he called out, stumbling for the living room. A curse tumbled from his lips for the arm

of the couch he slammed into, then he threw open the door.

Cody stood there, wide-eyed, and if Boone wasn't mistaken, terrified. He'd never seen his older brother scared before.

"Take my boy and keep him safe," Cody said in a desperate voice as he shoved his five-year-old son, Aaron, into Boone's arms.

The rattling of automatic gunfire echoed through the woods.

"What's happening?" Boone asked, scanning the woods as he clutched a whimpering Aaron tight to his chest.

"They've found us."

"Who?"

Cody backed off the front porch, and his piercing blue eyes dimmed with sadness. "Everyone."

Rory, Cody's mate, lay crumpled in the yard, her eyes fixed on him. "Boone, save him," she said in a hoarse whisper.

Adrenaline dumped into his veins as he raked his horrified gaze over her open stomach. Crimson stained her white sundress.

"Cody?" he uttered as he ripped his attention away

from Rory's suffering and searched his front yard. Cody had disappeared into the shadows as if he'd never existed at all.

"Run," his alpha's voice whispered on the wind.

Panting with panic, heart pounding against his sternum, Boone held Aaron tight against his chest and ran for the safety of the woods. This territory was his. He knew every nook and cranny, every rock crevice and cliff.

Branches whipped his face and shoulders as he ducked and dodged around them to protect Aaron. To the left, running parallel, Gage was herding his mate, Leah, and their two cubs in the same direction. Blue moonlight covered them in eerie shadows, but he knew their scent. They were his crew, and they were here, running with him toward safety.

"Where's Dade?" Boone yelled, his voice sounding hollow against the onslaught of peppering gunfire.

Gage didn't answer, didn't even turn his head.

Aaron was crying now, frail shoulders shaking. He hadn't hit his first growth spurt yet and was tiny still, in need of protection.

"It's okay," Boone panted out as his limbs became heavy. "You're safe with me, little bear." He hoped his

words sounded more confident than he felt.

He slowed, struggling against the waterlogged sensation his legs had adopted. His feet dragged through the pine needles that blanketed the forest floor, and when he turned to Gage to ask for help, a spray of bullets echoed through the wilderness and bowed Gage and his family forward with pained cries.

"Gage!" Boone yelled, desperation clawing at his throat.

Turning away in horror, he laid eyes on Ma, kneeling in the dirt, humming an off-key tune as she rocked back and forth, back and forth. She was hunched over something, so he dragged his heavy body closer and searched the ground in front of her. Dade and Bruiser lay beside each other, heads resting in Ma's lap, eyes clouded, staring vacantly into the space between them, faces smattered with blood. Quinn lay alone in front of them, white dress tattered and knees bloodied. She was struggling on her last breath, her lungs rattling with fluid.

"Oh, God!" Boone cried, shaking his head. "Ma, run!"

"Too late for me, my Boone. My heart died with my boys." A crack of gunfire sounded and Ma jolted

straight up, a look of shock and pain in her blue eyes. A red stain spread across her chest as she whispered, "Save her."

Her? Boone looked down in his arms, but he wasn't holding Aaron anymore. He was holding Cora.

"I'm scared," Cora whispered, blond hair whipping about in the wind, hazel eyes as round as the full moon.

"You should be," Shayna whispered from the shadows. "Boone brought you to the Reaper." She stepped out from behind a towering spruce tree, handgun trained on the woman in his arms.

"It's okay," Cora whispered just before Shayna pulled the trigger.

The sound of metal cracking against the firing pin was deafening, and Cora slid from his arms.

"Nooo!" he screamed, the word transforming into a roar.

Boone woke up yelling, throat hoarse, body rigid from fighting in his mind. His bedroom was dark, but the blue moonlight filtered through the open window as the chilly fall breeze brushed across his damp skin.

Supernatural electricity zinged up his arms and legs, sparking against his muscles until he seized.

Back arching against the tossed bed sheets, he began his Change just as the first whisper reached his ear.

"Laura will be so pissed she missed this," someone murmured, laughter in their voice.

Helplessly, Boone dragged his gaze to the window, where a cellphone camera showed a terrifying reflection of himself—veins bulging, skin ripping, fur sprouting, screaming...roaring.

Fury blasted through him in the final moments of his Change. He was a territorial hellion. These intruders had come onto his land, witnessed another one of his nightmares...the ones where he couldn't save the people he cared about. They saw him vulnerable. Recorded it to be replayed over and over again.

No. *No, no, no.*

Boone stood up on his hind legs and roared. Scared whimpers from the spies, and that was better. They should know.

Boone Keller was a monster—a death bringer—and they should see their end coming.

He dropped to all fours, claws raking against the carpet and lips curling back over his long canines.

And then he charged.

Want more of these characters?

Bear My Soul is the first book in a three book series called Fire Bears.

You can also read more about them in T. S. Joyce's Saw Bears series.

For more of these characters, check out these other books.

Bear My Soul
(Fire Bears, Book 1)

Bear the Heat
(Fire Bears, Book 3)

About the Author

T.S. Joyce is devoted to bringing hot shifter romances to readers. Hungry alpha males are her calling card, and the wilder the men, the more she'll make them pour their hearts out. She werebear swears there'll be no swooning heroines in her books. It takes tough-as-nails women to handle her shifters.

Experienced at handling an alpha male of her own, she lives in a tiny town, outside of a tiny city, and devotes her life to writing big stories. Foodie, wolf whisperer, ninja, thief of tiny bottles of awesome smelling hotel shampoo, nap connoisseur, movie fanatic, and zombie slayer, and most of this bio is true.

Bear Shifters? Check

Smoldering Alpha Hotness? Double Check

Sexy Scenes? Fasten up your girdles, ladies and gents, it's gonna to be a wild ride.

For more information on T. S. Joyce's work,
visit her website at
www.tsjoyce.com

Printed in Great Britain
by Amazon